WINNING HER

THOMPSON BROTHERS
BOOK ONE

SUMMER COOPER

LOVY BOOKS

Copyright © Lovy Books Ltd, 2018.

Summer Cooper has asserted her right under the Copyright, Designs and Patents Act 1988 to be identified as the author of this work.

This book is a work of fiction. Names and characters are the product of the author's imagination and any resemblance to actual persons, living or dead, is entirely coincidental.

In no way is it legal to reproduce, duplicate, or transmit any part of this document in either electronic means or in printed format. Recording of this publication is strictly prohibited and any storage of this document is not allowed unless with written permission from the publisher. All rights reserved.

Respective authors own all copyrights not held by the publisher.

Lovy Books Ltd
20-22 Wenlock Road
London N1 7GU

Cover by SC Creative

Matthew Thompson sat in his private room in front of a roaring fire. It was just another day, and he was ending it in comfort.

He should have been a happy man, quietly enjoying the fruits of his labors. But how could he when his children had all but abandoned him? Well, his sons at least; his daughter sat on a couch a few feet away from him, her feet tucked neatly under the chair. She was too busy with her phone to notice him and had been since they'd sat down to eat dinner.

As the last of his children still living with him, she could at the very least have been keeping him company, he noted sourly. And he didn't just mean her sitting there and doing her thing as he stared into the roaring fire, bored out of his mind. Why couldn't people have conversations anymore? Why did people only want to talk through a screen now?

He flicked a glance at his own phone, screen down just at his fingertips. He was so bored he couldn't even read.

He missed his children, the sound of laughter filling the air, the secret whispers as they plotted some mischief only children could get up to. He missed how when they were younger, they'd run up to him every time he came home, welcoming him with open arms. When was the last time that even happened?

Matthew was willing to settle for having them all in the same area.

After several more minutes passed and Emily didn't so much as look up, he sighed and called out to his daughter.

"Emily?"

"Hmm?" Her slim fingers flew over her phone's screen as she typed something out. She was the perfect blend of both him and his wife—a daughter a man could be proud of, if only she'd pay attention.

Matthew let out his heaviest sigh yet.

"Would you at least look up at your old man? I'm starting to feel a little jealous of your phone, here."

Her fingers slowed as she glanced up, but they didn't stop. He didn't even feel like sighing anymore.

"Do you need something, Dad?"

He rolled his eyes. "What I need is for you to sit up, put your phone down for a minute, and listen to your father. What happened to you, Emily? You used to be Daddy's little girl, and these days it's like you rarely have time to talk to me."

She flushed a little, her hands finally pausing on her

phone. She looked down at it for a few seconds before turning off the screen and putting it to one side.

"All right," she said, sitting upright, back straight, and hands placed demurely on her knees. "Although, Dad, it has been quite a few years since I was your 'little girl,' you know?" She arched a delicate eyebrow, bright eyes twinkling with a bit of mischief.

Matthew rolled his eyes. He could do that same eyebrow trick, his were just a bit grayer than hers.

"Anyway, what did you want to talk about?" At least she'd put the phone down now.

Matthew smiled, his tall frame and lined face so like his sons and his daughter. "I want you to help me plot how to get your brothers back here."

Her hands twitched on her knees in surprise. She flipped some blonde strands of hair that had fallen over her shoulder and blinked at him. That wasn't the reaction he was hoping for, but the one he'd counted on getting.

"Excuse me?" she said.

"I want my sons back, Emily. They might not have as much time for me, just like you, but can you even remember the last time they visited?"

She opened her mouth but paused because there was nothing she could say. It was true. The sons of the Thompson household hadn't been back for quite a while. During the holidays they tried to all meet up, but it wasn't in their family home where they'd all grown up.

"Can you manage it, though?" she said after a minute, frowning. "I mean, they're all busy doing who knows what wherever they are—"

"You don't know where they are?"

She looked offended. "Dad. I could tell you where Trent is. But the other two tend to move around a lot, so you're on your own there."

Matthew nodded. It was all he needed. Trent would have to be the first he called home because he was the most stable, the most put together. He would be easier to invite, though for many reasons he would be the hardest to get to stick around.

"Fine," he said, thumping his hand down on a knee. "Call him up. Give him whatever excuse, but I want to see him back here."

Emily flinched. "Dad! I never said I'd help you! I don't want any part of this scheme or whatever it is you're cooking up!"

Matthew chuckled. "You mean what *we* are cooking up," he corrected, ignoring her refusal. "Don't you want to help your aging father? Don't be so difficult, Emily. Help an old man out."

It didn't take much pleading to get her to cave. Even though she had grown, she was still his little girl in a lot of ways, and she loved to make her father happy. His daughter had always been such a warm, loving person, so as long as he hinted that he was unhappy, she would do something to change it.

He considered himself very lucky to have had her. She was the second most important woman in his heart after he'd lost his first wife.

"As much as I love traveling to meet up with your brothers, don't you think it would be best they come here?"

he needled. "Once they're all home, I can just relax my old bones, and they would be the ones to come to me for a change. Please, Emily."

Of course, Matthew wasn't as old and tired as he was trying to make himself out to be. He was getting on in years, but he still considered himself young and spry. He wasn't even in his sixties yet, and he was retired. But there was no reason to inform her of that just yet.

She was buying his ploy, and as much as a part of him felt bad that he was practically tricking his daughter, he was glad she was willing to help him out in this.

Matthew knew he would need it.

"Fine," Emily said with a sigh like he'd known she would. "I'll help. But if it doesn't go the way you plan, you'll be on your own, Dad."

Matthew just smiled, looking forward to having all his children together with him again. Finally.

1

TRENT

I walked into the office and heads turned in my wake. I didn't care if it was my height or my expensive suit that caught people's eyes, but I strutted across the room like I owned the place.

In a way, I did.

I walked over to the elevator and pressed the button to go up. A few people waited for one to come down to either of my sides, and I kept facing straight ahead as they turned to each other to mutter and gossip. I didn't bother listening to what they said. It was all the same.

They loved to talk about how I was smart, sophisticated, and savvy. That part, I loved to hear. I was totally in control of my world and my father's empire, and I didn't mind that people envied me for that.

The rumors I hated were the ones about how my father must have helped me get to where I was. That I'd spent all my life riding on his name and his money, instead of building up my own life and career without much of Dad's help. None of them knew the real me, or the life I'd endured to get where I am now. Still, no matter how much I hated hearing it, I never let those emotions show.

Be in control at all times.

That was the motto I'd set up for myself, and I'd followed it just fine over the years. So what if people talked shit behind my back? I was going to show them just what my effort brought me, and I was doing it my way.

The elevator doors finally opened and I walked inside. None of the other people waiting followed me in, and after a few seconds, the doors slid shut with only me inside.

Well.

Not that it was unexpected. I was the big boss around here, and most people naturally kept out of my way. None of that stopped them from gossiping about me, though.

As I was left alone, I swept my hand through my thick, blond hair and frowned to myself as I thought about cutting it short. It got in the way when it was long enough to fall over my forehead and tickle the nape of my neck. But I was too busy with work for even a quick trip to the high-priced salon I visited to have my hair cut.

The inside of the elevator was reflective, as though the walls were made of mirrors. I'd checked myself at home, but I didn't mind checking again. Everything had to be perfect and in place. The shined black shoes, pressed dark slacks and matching jacket, the navy-blue shirt under it and the blue and black striped tie were all perfectly in place without even a stray thread to mar the picture of perfection. I'd styled my hair away from my forehead and I pushed it back just a little more. I held my briefcase at my side, a gold diamond watch on my wrist and a small ring on my pinkie finger. I kept my right hand free of accessories because it was my dominant arm.

The elevator stopped on my floor, and I shrugged my shoulders to readjust how the jacket had settled, even though I knew it was already perfect. I strode onto the floor, heading straight for my office. There were fewer people here, but I still caught their attention.

My PA was already at her desk and working, and I gave a small nod of approval. I'd given her instructions the day she started working for me, and one of them was that she always be there earlier than me in the morning and be ready for anything I needed her to do. She stood up as I walked over to her desk, lifting a cup of take-out coffee from her desk and holding it out to me.

"Thank you, Jennifer," I said, accepting it.

I took a sip and almost sighed at the taste. I gave another small, near imperceptible nod of approval. Like she could see it, she beamed for a moment, then schooled her face to professional politeness.

"Please patch any important calls over to me," I instructed. "If it's not so important, please handle it yourself."

It was going to be a busy day, and we both knew it.

"Yes, sir," she said with a sharp nod.

I nodded back and walked over to my door, pushing it open with my shoulder. I moved over to my desk and set down the coffee and briefcase, then rounded it as I took off my coat. It was still a bit early, and the air hadn't quite warmed up yet, but I might as well be prepared early. I draped the coat over the back of my chair and sat down. I pulled some important documents out of my briefcase, then set it down to the side.

Finally, I took another sip of my coffee, cracked my fingers, and got down to work.

I had about twenty minutes to look over some papers; then the calls started coming in. My PA took care of some of them, but I still got the bulk of them, and I settled into the busy environment with ease, taking phone call after phone call and ending them with both sides satisfied.

It hadn't been easy starting out, but I'd made my fortune as a financial trader. Of course, there were plenty of people under the impression I got so many investors because of my father's connections. Quite the contrary, I'd distanced myself as much as I possibly could from the Thompson family name. There was the occasional investor who called me up because they saw my name and connected it to my dad's but as far as I cared, Thompson was just another name. Working with me didn't mean they would get any perks out of my dad.

Not that he would give perks to anyone, even his sons. My old man was nothing if not a proper businessman.

Most of the morning was spent taking calls, and by the time it hit lunch I was starting to feel the strain. I'd got used to being busy and it barely phased me anymore. I'd learned early on that you didn't get anywhere without hard work. I'd wanted to make a name for myself, with my time and my sweat, and I had.

My PA popped in with my lunch, and I barely gave her a grateful nod before going right back to work.

The calls were starting to grow less frequent in the afternoon. I caught some bites in between the calls, then tossed the remains of lunch into the trash can to my side behind the desk.

It was the usual, busy day. That was until my PA walked into my office, looking hesitant. I glanced up at her but finished the call I was on before giving her my full attention.

"Is there something wrong?" I asked, frowning. "Did you get a difficult client?"

She shook her head. "Um, not a client, sir. She says she's your sister? She's on another line for you."

My sister…

Emily.

My frown deepened. What could she possibly want from me?

"She's my half-sister," I grumbled to myself.

My PA shifted her weight from foot to foot, looking at me with partially concealed anxiety.

I rarely ever took personal calls in the office. I'd chosen Jennifer in particular to be my assistant, because she knew little of my background, and didn't look into it as long as it didn't help her do her job. She knew I had at least one brother, but that was it.

Seriously, though, what could Emily possible want?

"Just let her know I'm too busy," I said dismissively, waving at Jennifer. "Unless the calls have stopped coming?" I added, arching an eyebrow.

She winced. "Uh, no, actually, sir. There was a call that came in before hers; I promised you'd call back after you were done with your recent call. I just wanted to see if you'd be talking to your sister or not…"

"Tell her what I just told you," I said, already looking away.

Whatever Emily had to say to me, it could certainly wait until office hours were over. She and I weren't particularly close, and I couldn't remember the last time she even called me. It probably wouldn't be anything important.

But Jennifer wasn't leaving to go patch through my next call, and I looked back up at her with a frown. She had her hands clasped in front of her, though her fingers kept twisting, and she shifted slightly from one foot to the other some more. I wondered if the heels she was wearing were starting to feel uncomfortable on her feet.

"Is there something else I can help you with?"

"It's just that," she started slowly. "I'm sorry sir, but she said it had something to do with your dad."

My frown deepened even further. What could Dad possibly want from me? Even knowing it was about him, I still felt reluctant.

Right here was where I'd built my world. I'd all but thrown my past away because it was exactly what led me to where I was, in my new life in Asheville, North Carolina, where I could get away from it all. The place was perfect; no family in sight and I found my peace in the mountains I loved to hike. Where none of my dysfunctional family could butt in.

I still saw Dad on occasion because he'd gripe at me until I either met up with him or he'd show up at my office. The latter was something I didn't want to happen, so I usually gave into his demands. Come to think of it; it had been a while since I'd received as much as a call from him.

I'd been happy that he was finally leaving me alone.

Dad and I just didn't get along, no matter what the old man felt. He thought I was busy, but really I made whatever excuse kept me from going home. I hadn't been back for years, not since I left there for college.

I'd always wanted to leave after my mother died. She had pretty much been my world growing up because dad was always busy. Losing her had been a big blow, and what was worse was how quickly Dad found a woman to replace her. I was against him remarrying and he'd done it anyway. He gave all his affection to his new wife and the family she gave him, and I moved myself to the side, distancing myself before they had the chance to push me out.

My brothers were the only ones in the family I talked to with any regularity, and even then, they rarely wanted to talk to me because I'd made it clear I wanted out of the family's clutches.

Now, here was my sister, calling me over something to do with my father. It was just strange enough to have me curious.

I refocused on my PA who was still squirming in front of me and sighed as I waved a hand at her.

"Patch her through."

She looked visibly relieved as she left my office. A moment later, the phone at my desk rang. I took a deep breath to steel myself, before picking up the call.

"Hello?" I said, my voice coming out the same as if I was

taking a formal business call, the pitch just right to make a man think competence and a woman think of sins.

"Trent?" came the light voice. "It's me, Emily."

"What can I do for you, Emily?" I tapped a rapid beat on my desk with my fingers as I worked to keep my impatience out of my voice. She'd barely spoken, and already I wanted to cut the call.

"Sorry for calling you up at work," she said. You don't sound very apologetic to me, Emily, I thought to myself as she hesitated. "But I'm afraid it's something important. It's Dad."

I rolled my eyes. "Not everything to do with Dad has to be important, so you're going to have to be a little more specific than that. I am in the middle of my working day, and you're holding me up right now."

There was a short silence. When her voice came again, it was just a tad colder. Not too much though. I'd never heard Emily ever sound cold or angry, even as spoiled as she must have been, growing up the only daughter for Dad to dote on.

"You'll want to come back home for this, Trent. I know you can't be bothered with the rest of us but don't you at least care what's happened to him? Just come back home, Trent," she finished with a lilt of pleading at the end.

Why the fuck should I? I wanted to growl down the line. After everything I'd done to distance myself from my family, to act like I wasn't one of them… I was finally free of them. And now what? Just because she said so, I had to head back to Charlotte, the place I'd left all those years ago without a single glance back? Back to a life I'd wished for so long that I could leave behind, a name I'd wanted to leave behind.

It wasn't that I hated my father. If something were really up with the old man, it would worry me. The first few years when it was just me, Mom and Dad had been wonderful and the best years of my life. I did, however, resent all of Dad's choices ever since Mom passed away, and the demands he'd made on my life as if he had the right to just because he'd fathered me.

My life was mine to live how I wanted. I wasn't ready to give that up, even for my father.

"Trent?" Emily said, her voice questioning.

I was brought out of my revelry, and I realized I must have been silent for too long. I couldn't help myself. I was in control of everything else in my life, but this was something I couldn't do anything to change. When it came to my complicated family, it was so easy to forget myself.

"Yes?" I murmured to let her know I was still listening.

"Can't you come back?" she asked simply, but the question was far more complicated than any of them truly realized.

I kept my silence. If this was another of Dad's schemes to try and drag me back there… he was going to be so fucking disappointed.

"Dad had a heart attack," she said, at last, a note in her voice I'd never heard before. Was it desperation? Grief?

The words were dropped so suddenly, so quietly, that it took me a minute for the words to sink in. When they did, I felt my gut clench uncomfortably.

"I'm sorry, what?" I said, my voice tight, hoping I'd just misheard. "Dad had a what?"

"A heart attack," she repeated, her voice clear. "For this much, do you think you can finally come home? I know he'd want to see you, Trent."

When… how?

Those were the primary thoughts running through my brain. I wanted to say it was impossible, but when was the last time I'd talked to Dad? He'd been fine then, but I was pretty sure it was more than a year ago. It was a hard pill to swallow that a strong, proud man like my father could have had a heart attack. He worked himself hard but he'd always kept fit and healthy!

At least… as far as I'd seen, which I had to admit, wasn't much lately.

Well, fuck.

"Give me a day," I said to Emily, my voice a bit abrupt, but I didn't care.

Immediately, I cut the line, because I didn't want to hear whatever else she had to say. As much as I hadn't wanted to go back, I knew…

It's time.

2

JESSI

I hummed to myself as I moved through my space. The kitchen in the Charlotte branch of the Thompson Hotel chain was quite spacious, but with so many people working in it, it could feel pretty crowded at times.

It was a working environment I'd had to grow used to, but it was one I enjoyed thoroughly.

As usual, I had my phone in one of my pockets, my earbuds in, cords under my work clothes, and I was making another of my specialties.

Working as a pastry chef wasn't the easiest thing in the world. Working as a pastry chef at one of the best-known hotels in the country was even harder. It was pretty demanding, and there was no room for mistakes. But I'd proven myself when I was hired, and I'd become one of the top pastry chefs in the Thompson Hotels.

I was just finishing the layout for one of my cakes.

Everyone else went about their own business at their own workstations, and no one bothered me as I worked.

Well, no one but my mother anyway.

The call was unexpected enough to startle me, and I glanced around to make sure no one had noticed. The calm music I was listening to was suddenly the loud song I'd set as my ringtone. I checked my phone, and sure enough, her name was right there.

She was the only person that still called me during work hours. But she was my mom, so I could hardly tell her to stop calling me, no matter how distracting it got. I hurried through the parts that couldn't wait, before picking up the call just before it was dropped.

"What can I help you with, Mom?" I asked, not leaving out the exasperation from my voice.

"Did I distract you from work again?" It was always her first sentence when I'd answer a call.

I wanted to roll my eyes, but if I did it every time my mom asked the same question, my eyes would ache in their sockets.

"It's fine, Mom. What did you call me for?"

I glanced at the work I'd done so far, mentally going through what I would need to do to have a perfect standing cake in front of me. After that came the slicing, then the decorating.

"Honey," Mom said, voice turning conspiratorial, catching my attention. "You'll never believe what happened. It's just horrible! Mr. Thompson had a heart attack!"

I gasped, my mind now fully on my mom's news. It was

huge. It had been a while since I'd seen Mr. Thompson in person but it was hard to imagine he'd had a heart attack. He'd always seemed larger than life, even when I got to see a side of him most wouldn't see.

"When did it happen?" I asked, keeping my voice hushed.

The last thing I needed was someone getting curious about what I was talking about. None of my coworkers knew the background I had with the Thompsons, and I didn't want to make waves where I worked.

"I'm not sure, but it couldn't have been that long ago. All the sons are finally coming home to see their father's condition. If we want more information, it would have to come after that."

Wait… what? The Thompson sons were all coming back to Charlotte?

"I'm sorry, Mom, but what did you say?" I asked slowly, wishing she would say something other than what she'd said.

"Mr. Thompson's sons are all coming back home," she repeated carelessly, not aware of how each word dug into my heart like an ice pick. "Isn't that wonderful, honey? I was starting to get worried about that man left in that big house with just his daughter to look after him."

No, Mom. It's not wonderful. It's the exact opposite.

I thought the words but didn't dare say them out to my mother in case she asked me why. Because that was something I couldn't tell her. There was little of my life that I hadn't told my mom about, but this was one thing I'd thought best to keep to myself. I wanted the moment to have never happened, and I'd tried to live acting as if it hadn't.

And what did she mean about Mr. Thompson being lonely? It was a big house, sure, but it was full of servants that saw to the man's every need.

My parents had been in that position all of my life, servants to one of the richest men in the world.

"Um, look, Mom. I need to be getting back to work, alright? I don't want anything to burn. I'll talk to you when I get off?"

She sighed. "Fine, honey. I'll be waiting!"

I hung up, thinking hard about how I didn't want to have to call her back so that she could tell me the last thing I wanted to hear all over again.

Why did they have to come back?

Not that I particularly had a thing against them all. It was just one of them that I had a problem with.

Growing up, I'd been in the Thompsons' shadow. Both of my parents had worked for the family pretty much since before I was born. My mom, Joan, worked as a house-keeper while my dad, Ted, worked as the family butler. Through them, there were some occasions where I'd get to see Mr. Thompson, though those times were few. More recently, I'd met him after I started working at this hotel.

But even though I'd grown up in their shadow, I was growing out of it. I wasn't just a child of the house help; I was making a name for myself with my work, my creations.

The father had been good to my parents. He wasn't like what most TV shows made rich, successful businessmen out to be. He was pretty respectful of his staff, and he'd never said a bad word to either of my parents as far as I knew. In fact, they sang his praises.

It was Trent Thompson, the oldest son of the house, who I had a problem with. My chest was filled with dread at just the thought of him stepping back into the city, and I hadn't seen him yet.

What was I going to do?

Memories started to resurface, memories of my childhood. Memories of the crush I'd always had on Trent. They were sweet in the beginning, all young and full of curiosity. He was already quite a character back then, but my crush had only persisted, until one day he'd figured it out.

He'd laughed. I was still traumatized by that. When you're a young girl, even when you're shy and nervous with a boy you like, you don't picture them laughing at your feelings like they meant nothing, but that was exactly what Trent had done to me.

Afterward, he'd even gone to talk to his father because of it. He didn't just talk bad about me though. No. He'd tried to talk his father into letting my parents go, firing them as a punishment for me. I figured he must have thought the only reason I was after him was because of the family money.

Back then, more than because he'd laughed, that he thought that money was the extent of my interest in him had hurt me immensely. Being laughed at was humiliating, but not as painful as my love for him being dismissed as a love for his money.

It stuck with him. When I struck up a friendship with

his half-sister Emily, he'd shown how much he resented it, like in his mind I was getting near her because I'd missed my chance with the first born and heir, so I was endearing myself to the sole daughter of the family who pretty much got whatever she wanted if it wasn't too outrageous. Although, "outrageous" meant different things to the rich than it would to everybody else.

Things between Emily and me were hardly like that, though. Emily loved food, a love that I shared. It had been enough to get me through culinary school. When I'd come back as a chef, Emily couldn't have been more delighted, and it had remained our bond.

Back when I still lived in the mansion, before I'd left for college, Emily would sneak into the staff quarters. She'd always been a curious, happy child, and everyone loved her so no one ever gave away her secret even after she was caught. It was how she and I had officially met for the first time. I taught the young, rich girl who had everything handed to her with a word or the snap of her father's fingers how to cook in the small kitchen in my parent's shared quarters at the mansion. After that, she'd sneak downstairs and we'd play chef. I told her one day that I would become a real chef.

I'd kept that promise, and Emily and I were still as close as ever. Even though I didn't get to see her much because work was so demanding. But on the days I had the time, she'd show up in the hotel kitchens, and we'd make something, pretend it was like old times.

"Jessi!"

I jumped with an aborted yelp, eyes widening as my

mouth fell open, and I turned to the person who'd just shouted my name and nearly stopped my heart from beating, cutting off my trip down memory lane in the process.

"Laura!" I said her name chidingly. "You didn't have to scare me like that!"

She just rolled her eyes. "Well, I'm sorry, but you've just been standing there staring off into space for a while, you know? Someone already did the work for the cakes."

I looked over to where I'd left my work and frowned to realize the space had been cleared already. Yeah, I wasn't the only pastry chef there, but usually people didn't just come and hijack my work. I needed it, dammit! I needed to have something there to keep me busy, to stop me from thinking, and to help me put off talking to my mom for as long as possible.

My eyes narrowed at Laura. She was a colleague of mine, though she didn't work in the same area I did.

"What did you even call me for?"

"I just wanted to let you know that we're pretty much done for the day. There are other people that will be dealing with setting the food up for clients. The pastry chefs can go home."

What? No!

I didn't yell out like I wanted to, but it was a close call.

"Are you sure there isn't anything else for me to do?" I asked, and I was sure I sounded a little desperate, but I didn't care. "I could start up on the menu for tomorrow, at least make some dough and put it in the fridge so I won't have to start from scratch tomorrow…"

"You already did that," she said impatiently, frowning. "Don't you remember?"

Ah. "I'd just forgotten," I said sheepishly. "Sorry about that."

Laura rolled her eyes, but there was a trace of worry around them even as she frowned at me.

"Is there something you'd like to tell me?" she asked.

I bit down on my lip, indecisive. On the one hand, having someone to vent to would be wonderful. I'd done it back when I was a student and things got hard, and it had helped. On the other hand, this was something so private I worried about just blurting it out. Laura and I were friends as well as colleagues but she didn't know everything there was to know about me. There might be the relief of someone else knowing, but...

Even if she were a friend, I'd have to relive the humiliation to tell her all about it. That was something I was not willing to put myself through, even to get this huge secret off my chest.

"Nothing, really," I murmured, my eyes sliding away from hers because I didn't like lying to her. "I'm just thinking a little too much, that's all. You don't need to worry."

She watched me for a while in silence. I knew she knew I was lying, but as long as she wouldn't call me out on it, I was going to ignore it.

"Whatever you say," she said dismissively after what felt like a whole minute. "But you should probably go and see to whatever that call was. It's obviously something important. You're not acting like yourself. I've never seen you just stop in the middle when you're baking."

I took a deep breath then released it slowly, sending her a grateful look for not prying, even as I dreaded what I was going to walk into in a little while.

"You're right," I muttered. "Absolutely. It was… something important."

It was the last thing I wanted, but I started undoing my uniform.

"I'll see you tomorrow," she shouted at me as I walked towards the employee area.

I was too distracted by my thoughts and worries for a verbal reply, but I waved at her over my shoulder.

A side door in the kitchen led into the staff area. I moved over to my locker and switched my chef's uniform for my overcoat before picking up my purse. Then I made my way out of the hotel using the staff entrance and exit.

I might as well go help my mom out because I knew she might need to prepare for the return of the prodigal sons.

I just need to keep my feelings about Trent to myself, I thought, hoping it was possible. Hell, I might not see him at all… I'm busy, and he probably would be as well…

I was just trying to placate myself. No matter how busy we both were, I was close friends with Emily, and my parents still worked at the family mansion. That he and I would run into each other was very likely.

My mind jumped back into the past, and I remembered his laughter. The bitter heartache of it—just the memory of it—made my cheeks burn, even now when I was an adult and I knew my worth. I wasn't the same insecure teenage girl with her first crush; I was a grown woman with a career who'd set a path for herself.

I can't forget the past, I thought to myself with a sigh. I doubted I ever would, no matter how many years passed. And seeing Trent in the flesh for the first time in years would just make it all the harder for me.

Then there was a hopeful thought.

I've grown since then, so he must have as well, right? Maybe he'd grown past the smarmy teenager that laughed when I declared my love for him and wiped his kiss away.

A girl could dream, couldn't she?

3

———

TRENT

I left work an hour after talking to Emily and drove home, where I packed a small bag before starting on the journey back home, to Charlotte.

Damn, I'd hoped I'd never had to go back there.

There was a reason I hadn't been back since high school, but this was something important.

Please, I thought. Let nothing happen to Dad.

The extent of my worry surprised me a little. My dad and I hadn't been close in quite a while. I could barely remember the times when I loved and respected him like a father without any smudges getting in the way. That had been gone a while ago.

But here I was putting my whole life on hold. On hold, because I knew what I was going to do once I got home. Yeah, I already did work for my dad and his empire, but I also had my separate career. I'd spent time building it, and I was leaving it like it was nothing.

There was no way to know how long this was all going

to take. I'd left Jennifer with a lot of work to do, and I'd be immersed in running things for my dad soon. I knew just how much work he had on his plate because I still remembered how he'd stay out late more often than not, and when he did get back, he looked exhausted.

Nothing is going to happen to him, I thought to myself, wanting to make it through if I had to use sheer force of will. I'll get there, and he'll be just fine, asking me why this was the first time I was visiting in so long, and saying what a bad son I am.

It didn't make the clench around my heart ease, and after a while I decided to put on some music, hoping it would distract me.

After hours of steady driving on some rather bone-crushing roads and a few stops on the way to catch something to eat and stretch my legs, I made it home. Dad's mansion was located on the outskirts of Charlotte. It was this huge, brick thing of marble columns and three floors, shaped like an angular 'c', with two wings on each side. It was visible from a distance, and I couldn't help scoffing at it. Most people would look at it and see a beautiful house, but all I saw was a prison I was willingly taking myself into.

"It hasn't changed at all, has it?" I muttered to myself, feeling a little awed.

More than a decade had passed and this place still looked timeless. I could remember distant memories of Mom and me coming back home after we'd gone out to have fun just the two of us because Dad was always so busy. There were few times when he ever joined in.

This house… it had been my hell and my haven in my formative years.

It was pretty big for three people, though after Dad remarrying I'd felt stifled in there, even though it was the one place with the happiest memories of my mom in it.

A lot of people were under the impression it was my father's name that brought me so many clients. I'd launched my career years ago, but it had picked up pretty quickly. A couple of years after I'd started out I was on my way to the top. I knew people who'd started earlier than I did were still struggling to make ends meet.

People had way too many false impressions about me.

It was this place that had given me the drive I needed to get out from under my father's thumb, to escape the stifling atmosphere. I had a good dose of my mom's charm and intelligence, to go with it, which helped.

This mansion was the place I shared memories with my mom. Yet not long after she was gone, all these strangers were coming out of nowhere and making their happy memories when my mom was dead.

I'd resented them all for being happy. Even while I'd known that wasn't completely fair of me. But I'd been so lost in my pain back then that I didn't care, and I was too old to be thinking of starting anything with my family anymore.

When I pulled up to the gate, I was ready to call in to have the doors unlocked, but they pulled open without my having to do anything. I arched an eyebrow, somewhat impressed by the tech Dad must have invested into his home. I'd told Emily I would arrive tomorrow, but I'd changed my plans as Dad's condition finally sank in and I'd realized I might have little time to waste.

In my mind, my place was nothing compared to the mansion. It was just enough space for me to live comfortably, while pleasant enough for the occasional company. It wasn't too far from the office, and not too far from the mountains either.

I aimed the car down the long driveway, taking deep breaths to settle myself internally. No one here needed to know that I was the least bit ruffled. I didn't particularly care what they thought anyway, but the fact I'd appeared should have been enough to show that I cared.

Let's just get inside and see him first, I told myself. Worry about whatever else later.

And there would be a lot to worry about.

I parked the car a short distance from the massive front doors that were usually left open during daylight hours. I got out of the car with a grin, a rather self-satisfied one, picking my sports coat up from the back seat and putting it on. I didn't want to give the help the wrong impression. It just simply wouldn't do to have them thinking I was slouching.

I was a grown-up, and I was a successful businessman in my own right. It had been the right decision to leave this house, and I wanted them to know it. I cared what they thought less than what my dad thought, but I had an image to keep up.

I headed for the house, jogging up the short flight of stairs to the entrance. I walked inside, breezing past Ted. He was the family butler and had been for as long as I could remember. Though I hadn't paid much attention to the help growing up, I'd paid attention to him, because he was Jessi's father.

Jessi.

Another person I hadn't thought much of once I'd left. Idly, I wondered if I'd be running into her again.

I walked into one of the salons, looking for Emily. Luckily, I found her in the first one I walked into. She was lounging on a couch, her legs up and curled under her, her hair falling on either side of her face as she frowned down at the phone in her hand.

"Hey," I called, more to get her attention than an actual greeting, but it was enough to get her to look up, eyes slightly widened in surprise.

Wow, was the first thing I thought when I saw her. She's grown. Then, we look alike.

I frowned slightly at the obvious implications. She looked just as much like me as my brothers. Hair and eye color might differ between us, but besides that, we must have taken after my father. I'd gotten more of my looks from the old man than I liked. A part of me had wanted to think that I had something in me that resembled my mother. But clearly, Dad's genes were just too strong.

How had I not realized it before?

"Trent!" she yelped, scrambling to get off the couch and stand up.

I wondered what she was so surprised about. Wasn't she the one that called me and insisted I come back home?

"What is it?" I asked. "You wanted me home, and I'm

here." I held my arms out and open, before letting them fall back to my sides.

"Um, that's right," she murmured, fidgeting. "You're here. But you're not supposed to be here until tomorrow, you said!"

I watched as she looked anywhere but at me, her eyes moving in my general direction, but skittering away when they got anywhere near looking right into mine. She tucked her hair behind her ear on one side, then smoothed down her hair on the other. Her other hand was wrapped around her phone tightly enough her knuckles were white.

I frowned at her when I realized that she looked, nervous. Or, more like she looked afraid. Of me.

Fuck.

For a moment, I felt bad. Why was she acting as if some monster had come home? She was the one to call me back in the first place! Was there any need to look like I was going to eat her?

But the moment passed, and I just felt annoyed.

What the hell?

Did she have any reason to be acting that way around me? I'd been distant from Emily most, second only to her mother. I'd been nearly a teenager by the time she was born, and around that time I didn't even spend all that much time at home. I had no interest in playing with the new baby in the family. She'd still been young when I left, and I'd only seen her on a few occasions since then when dad would sometimes bring her on one of his visits.

The last time I saw her, she was just going through puberty. There was some resemblance, but the young woman standing in front of me looked almost nothing like the gangly girl I'd met last. After that, Dad had stopped dragging her along and I hadn't spoken to her face-to-face since then.

Was it because of that? Because we were meeting for the first time in a long while that she was acting so strangely? I was pretty sure I'd never been cruel to her, though I couldn't say I'd ever been welcoming. Most of the time I was just dismissive of her presence. That didn't exactly instill fear in anybody. Of everyone, she should probably be the one to feel nothing at my sudden arrival back home.

But then a thought occurred to me.

"Did something happen?" I asked, my voice tight.

She did that thing again where her eyes would rise to meet mine, only to stop halfway, and she'd end up looking over my shoulder instead. Why couldn't she meet my eyes?

"What do you mean?" she asked.

I wondered if I was mistaking the slight tremble in her voice.

"I mean, did something happen to do with Dad?" I asked, voice growing impatient. "He had a heart attack, did his condition get worse? Can you tell me where he is, so I can see him? I forgot to get the details from you before, so I just came all the way here."

She fidgeted some more, chewing down on her lower lip.

"You want to know about Dad, huh?" she muttered, finally meeting my eyes.

I frowned. "Yes. Where is he?"

She looked away, her hand rising once more to play with her hair nervously. My frown only deepened the longer she made me wait, and I wondered why she was so unwilling to answer me.

Why, after calling me back, was she suddenly getting possessive over Dad? Maybe she didn't want me to see him, even in the state he must have been in? Or... was Dad's state so bad that she was deliberately trying to keep me away from it?

It could be either one, and it didn't look like this girl was going to tell me! I felt like if I had to wait much longer I'd go mad or get angry enough to start shouting, and then she'd have something to look all frightened about.

"Can you please just tell me?" I asked one more time.

"Um," she floundered, waving a hand in the air between us. "You just got back, though! Aren't you tired, or anything? Did you bring any luggage with you? You could have it sent upstairs, maybe freshen up and have a meal... You must have been on the road for a while to get here this early in the day..."

I'd been on the road for hours, though I'd taken a stop at a cafe on the way to rest because I didn't want to end up with a broken back from those roads. Still, I'd only caught four hours of sleep the night before and it was tough getting back on the road again. I'd been worried the entire time too that I wasn't going fast enough. That by the time I arrived at the hospital it would be too late. It was only as I drove into Charlotte and saw the sign for the first hospital that I realized I had no idea where to go. Charlotte had no shortage of hospitals and Dad could be in any of them. I'd driven to the house hoping Emily could give me an answer when she didn't answer her phone.

And here I was, and this girl was refusing to answer my questions.

"You know what? I'm a busy man, Emily. I would like to see my father before anything else. Then I'm going to work on what needs to be done while he rests. So if you won't tell me, I'll find out on my own."

I went to turn away, but her voice stopped me.

"Wait, Trent!"

I paused, slowly turned back to her to wait for what she had to say. I wasn't there to play some waiting game with her when there were more important things to do, but I would indulge her this once. Frankly, the girl could probably do with a little less indulgence in her life.

"Well?" I prompted when she still said nothing.

"Are you sure you don't want something to eat?" she asked.

I rolled my eyes, at the end of my patience, and left the salon. Getting information on my father myself wouldn't be hard.

But I didn't see where I was going as I walked out the room and bumped into someone. Or rather, a smaller, soft body bumped into mine. She gave a small yelp as we collided, and I held her by the tops of her arms until she righted herself.

"Sorry about that," she said. "I didn't see where I was going—"

She looked up into my face, then cut herself off as she recognized who I was. I knew who she was, too.

Jessi.

Emily wasn't the only woman who'd grown around here. The last time I saw Jessi, she'd been this awkward, gangly girl, not unlike what Emily was like as in her early teens. I could hardly see that same person in her now.

But she was staring at me with her eyes wide and jaw dropped.

Another woman was looking at me like she'd seen a ghost. At least she was looking at me, and not through or around me. But this was Jessi, not my half-sister whom I had an awkward half-sibling relationship with. On the contrary, we had no relationship. None at all.

I took a moment to get a good look. Jessi had grown into a beautiful woman.

Just when did that happen?

4

————

JESSI

I was on my way out of the main part of the mansion and heading out when I saw the sense in my mom's words. I'd helped my mom with her work, and she'd even insisted I spend the night because by the time we were done with everything it was too late for me to have gone home. I turned around, my exhaustion telling me to stay.

It was a mistake.

I knew it even as I agreed with Mom's suggestion, and I sure as heck was regretting it now.

Of all the people... of all the times... why did it have to be Trent?

I knew I must have looked like an idiot, just standing there and acting like I'd seen a ghost or something. It was rude, and as soon as it occurred to me I tried to shift my expression to something polite, my lips trembling a little as the corners turned up in a smile.

"Hello," I said, at the very least trying to be civil.

Trent didn't even bother with that. As soon as I opened my mouth and spoke, he just frowned at me and stormed off.

Maybe he was in a hurry, I tried to tell myself. It had absolutely nothing to do with me.

But then I heard him muttering to himself as he walked off, not even bothering to keep his voice quiet.

"Servants using the front entrance now... my how things have changed around here..."

The words left me stricken, but by the time I turned around, he was already out of sight.

Fuck! Damn you, Trent!

It had been years. Fucking years, and yet he was still the one person that could make me feel smaller than an ant with just a few callous words. If anyone else had said those words, it would have been easy to brush them off. They could have been jealous or their dislike of me would have been petty. I didn't know exactly how Trent felt about me, but everything he said hit me harder than words from other people.

Just what the fuck had I been doing in all those years we'd been apart? I should have used it to get over this bastard.

Mood completely ruined, I turned back around. I didn't want to head the direction he'd gone. The chances we'd bump into each other twice were low, but I didn't want to risk it. Feeling incredibly stung, I headed back to my mom's apartment in the servants' wing.

You shouldn't still feel like this, I chided myself as I felt old wounds tearing open. What exactly did you expect, anyway? You knew it would be bad!

And I had known. I'd had it in my mind to keep away from Trent as much as was humanly possible for the duration of his stay. It probably wouldn't be long anyway; he'd always been itching to leave, so I doubted he'd come back to stay. As soon as Mr. Thompson was back on his feet and was able to do his work, Trent would probably leave.

Good riddance, I thought, but it was weak.

"Honey? You're back already?"

I looked up at my mom as I walked into the apartment. It was pretty spacious especially since it was part of the servant's quarters, the place I'd grown up in. The Thompsons were nice enough to provide their servants with good living. Our family's apartment consisted of a normal sized living room, two bedrooms, two bathrooms, and a cooking area. Not that we cooked much since there were always leftovers from Thompson's meals to eat.

It was like we had our own small house within the mansion. When I was younger, I still hadn't grasped the difference between our small space and most of the mansion that belonged to the Thompsons.

"Hey, Mom," I said, giving her a wan smile. "I'm back. Sorry to bother you again today."

I was trying my best to keep up appearances, but damn, was it hard. I wasn't sure if it was something in my face or my voice that gave me away, but Mom looked slightly alarmed like she could tell I wasn't really fine with just a glance.

"What's wrong?" she asked. "Did something happen? You've barely been out of this room for five minutes…"

It would be better if I didn't mention to her that I'd met Trent at all. Let alone that the drop in my mood was because of him. I'd have to explain a bit more, and I was going to keep my crush on Trent a secret from my mother for as long as possible.

"It's nothing, really," I said dismissively. "I just saw the sense in your words. I might as well stay a little longer, there's nothing wrong with it after all."

She pursed her lips, but I knew she was pleased. "You know I can't stay here to look after you, right? I'm going to be heading to bed. We'll have a very busy day tomorrow."

I shrugged. It wasn't like I needed a babysitter. "I just thought I should get some sleep, Mom, you don't have to worry so much. Work doesn't start for a few more hours and I don't need to go back to my place just to rest when I could stay right here."

Mom frowned at me. "You were in such a hurry to be on your way, though. Do you need me to get you something?"

I rolled my eyes. "Mom, no need to worry. Just go to bed, okay? Aren't you totally exhausted by now?"

Her eyebrows shot up as she glanced at the watch around her wrist. It was one Dad had saved up to buy for her on their third anniversary. I was surprised the watch even still worked.

"You're right, I need to get going. My sleeping pill is already starting to work." She walked over to me, caught me by the tops of the arms, and pecked a quick kiss on my cheek. "Get some good rest, all right? You look terrible, Jessi. Try not to overwork yourself, all right?"

I just nodded and waited for her to leave the room, though I could have told her I loved my job, and it was more relaxing for me more than anything. I didn't even mind the crazy hours I had to keep, some days getting up extra early, some days staying extra late.

The moment she was out, I couldn't keep up the façade. I'd been hiding my tears from her, but once I was alone, I could feel my eyes start to sting. I sniffled and tilted my head up as I blinked, refusing to let even a single tear fall.

That bastard…

He hadn't changed at all, had he? If anything, I'd have to say Trent had got worse since the time I'd known him. At least before, he wouldn't have acted like that. Not that he would have been nicer, but some verbal acknowledgment was better than getting a frown, then him walking away from me.

"What the fuck did I ever do to you, anyway?" I muttered to myself as I moved over to the couch and plopped down. "Besides making the stupid decision of loving you…"

It had to be one of the dumbest things I'd ever done. Trent obviously still thought so. I could feel my old resentment rise the more I thought about it.

Just… what the fuck? Because his father had money, did he have to be such an aloof asshole? It might have got a few girls to turn their heads back in high school, but it annoyed me now as it had then because now I wasn't looking at him through rose-tinted glasses. Not entirely, anyway.

I was no longer the naïve teenage girl with thoughts of healing the hurting bad boy. Because I could remember a time when he hadn't always been like that.

I sighed to myself and grabbed one of the pillows on the couch and hugged it to my chest.

How long has it been? I mused to myself. The time since he wasn't like that...

My parents had worked for his family long before I was born. I was pretty much raised in the mansion, just like all the Thompson kids, only in a different wing from it that they barely ever paid attention to, besides the ever-curious Emily.

Trent and I had known each other from the time we were born. So I'd seen what he was like before he suddenly changed.

Back when we were young, I'd attributed the change to the loss of his mother. He was such a happy child it was hard to think he'd grown up to be the asshole I knew today. Everything changed when he was around five and his mother passed away though. Since his dad was so busy, she was the person he'd spent most of his time around, and with her gone it was like he'd lost himself.

Abruptly, his attitude started to change. Once upon a time, he was happy and friendly, but then he grew gloomy and started to isolate himself. His attitude grew worse. When he interacted with others, even with me, he acted more snobbish than he had before, and it only got even worse as he aged.

When I first realized I had a crush on him, I was in my pre-teens. I'd had fantasies back then, that maybe there was a hole in his life, which was why he was acting as he did, and I could be the one to fill that hole his mother had left. I would be the one to soothe the anger he felt toward his step-mother, who ended up replacing his mom in his small family. I saw how he distanced himself from his family after that. He wouldn't let his step-mom anywhere near him after she had her first child with his dad—a son at that.

I imagine Trent probably felt like he was being replaced. He'd isolated himself from his family, and from her most of all.

I winced just thinking about it. I couldn't comprehend just what he felt because it was foreign to me. I'd only ever had my parents growing up, and no siblings. My parents had been kept by their duties a lot of the time, and I'd come to know pretty early on that they couldn't look after me all the time.

The thought had pushed me to gain some independence. I didn't want to depend so much on them because it felt like I was just a burden to them.

Still, there was never a time when I thought that I wasn't loved equally by both of my parents, even when we didn't get to see a lot of each other.

I let out an explosive sigh, coming to a decision.

"I'll have to keep helping Mom when she needs me," I muttered. "I can't exactly get out of that. I just have to stay out of his way."

I wasn't a servant at the Thompson mansion, but I knew where all the servant entrances were and I could go back to using them like I had when I was a kid. Emily would notice, but I could always just give her some excuse.

I decided to completely work Trent out of my system. There was nothing else I could do, was there?

Childish fantasies and whims aside, even if I could somehow get him to let me in, there was no way I'd be able to heal a man who was so full of himself and his anger that he forgot the rules of common courtesy.

It was probably pointless, and more importantly, I couldn't do that to myself. I drifted into sleep, the quiet of the house a balm to my aching soul.

5

———

TRENT

*F*uck. That was a bad move, Trent.

I knew what I was doing, even as I did it. But somehow, watching Jessi trying to pick herself up after she'd just given me a look like she was horrified was something I'd wanted to walk away from. There were better ways I could have done it—less harsh ways.

Why had I even said that? As if ignoring her wasn't bad enough! I'd wanted to bang my head against the nearest wall because I knew there was no way she wouldn't have heard me. And I'd hurt her deliberately.

But I couldn't stop myself. Old habits die hard and all that bullshit.

I could remember what our teen years were like. Even though I hadn't thought of her in a long while, the memories came to me with such clarity. I could even remember the last time I'd talked to her. I remembered down to the last detail of what she'd been wearing and how she'd done up her hair.

And afterward, her broken-hearted expression after I'd left her.

Fuck, but I'd been an asshole back then. I haven't changed much from that, have I?

I'd wanted to turn back as soon as I'd said those harsh words, but I'd forced myself to keep walking. Because I wasn't sure what I would have told her anyway.

Plus, there was the fact she'd changed. And not just a little bit, but a lot! That she was suddenly so breath-taking didn't help, and I wasn't sure I could talk to her without staring at her body, and that would be inappropriate. She'd offered me her heart on a platter, and I'd tossed it back in her face. There was no need to confuse the poor girl by suddenly acting all interested.

Besides, she was beautiful now; so what? I'd had my pick of the most beautiful women in the world, there was no reason why Jessi of all people should have my mind all muddled just from one look at her. I didn't need a pastry chef to fulfill my sexual needs. And the only reason I even knew her current occupation was because Dad had brought her name up a couple of times and mentioned it. I wasn't sure when it happened but for some reason, it had stuck with me.

Or maybe it was just because this was Jessie. Besides Dad and the older servants who'd stayed at the mansion forever, she was the only other person who remembered my mother had existed. My step-mom and half-siblings... I wasn't sure if they'd ever seen her in pictures. Dad hadn't got rid of them, but he'd moved all of the pictures of Mom we had hanging around, insisting instead that they be locked up somewhere he wouldn't have to see them unless he went looking for them.

I would visit that room sometime during my stay. I'd taken some pictures of Mom when I'd left but I didn't have nearly enough.

I planned to put Jessi out of my mind very quickly. Even though when I first saw her after so long, I'd felt a twinge of desire, unlike anything I'd ever felt before with any other woman.

Maybe it had been too long since I'd been with someone, I rationalized to myself. I'd been working for months on end now, using my hand for relief. After the whole deal with Dad was done, I promised myself I'd go looking for someone. It wouldn't take me long to find the companionship I needed.

Besides all that, I needed to focus on the current problem I found myself in. Because for all I knew, my dad could be dying somewhere, and my nitwit of a sister wasn't very forthcoming with information. I wanted to know which hospital he'd been taken to. There were quite a few within the area, but I could always go to the nearest and start asking from there. I would ask the staff, but if Emily was keeping quiet on it, they probably didn't know.

I suddenly just wanted to get out of the house. I didn't want another chance encounter with Jessi.

I might as well unpack. I went back for the suitcase I'd left in the trunk of my car. Ted, who was still waiting at the door, held his hand out in silent offering to carry my bag for me. I just shook my head and walked past him. Like I'd let an old man carry my luggage for me when I could do it just fine.

I wasn't sure which room I was supposed to take, but my feet moved on their own. I went up the stairs to the second floor and strode down the hallway until I stopped at a specific door. I stared at it for a moment, before reaching out and pushing it open. It was unlocked. When I looked inside, nothing had changed.

Seriously.

There was no thick smell of dust in the room, so someone must have at least cleaned it. But they could have made some changes. The room looked exactly as I'd left it when I went off to college. Shit, that was more than a decade ago.

Was this supposed to make me feel guilty?

I walked into the room feeling suspicious. I set my suitcase down, then walked around the room just a little. It should be impossible that no one had touched or moved anything in there. My memory wasn't so impeccable that I would remember every detail, but as far as I could tell, nothing had moved. It was bringing back some memories for me that I would have rather remained buried.

After the quick tour around my room, I dragged the suitcase over to the bed. At least the bed was made, something I didn't remember from when I'd left the room for the last time. This was worse, though, as if whoever left it like this had been waiting for me to come home.

I opened my suitcase and started pulling out clothes an item at a time. It was a pretty big suitcase with quite a few outfits, but for an impromptu trip of an unknown length of time, I'd packed lightly.

Once I had everything arranged on the bed I started moving them over to the closet, trying not to wrinkle anything. I hurried and was done in a matter of minutes. It was calming for my mind as well, and I didn't feel quite so unsettled afterward.

I left my room, feeling like I could go start looking for my dad now. I wasn't sure yet if I was going to go to the closer hospitals in the area or just track their numbers down before leaving. There was impatience growing in my chest because I still didn't know the state my father was in. A large part of me was still greatly worried.

I was headed for my car the moment I got outside but I never made it. Instead, I heard a car approaching and looked up in surprise.

What the hell...?

It was a private ambulance coming up the drive. There was only one reason I could think of for it to be here. Either it was coming to take my father or bringing him back. Whichever one, I didn't know why the vehicle had to be there. If Dad was feeling unwell, he should have been at the hospital already, and if he was there then he should stay there, not come back home.

I was holding my car door open when the ambulance stopped several feet away, closer to the door. I walked over, my fists clenching at my sides.

Damn it, Dad! Why aren't you in the hospital?

The back of the ambulance opened up, and I went over to greet my dad. A couple of people in white hospital outfits jumped out, and I could feel my fingers clench a little tighter. No one had told me what exactly had happened to him anyway, and my mind was to the point of making things up on its own.

It had to be bad, right? Or someone would have just told me. I slowed to a stop beside the ambulance. I wanted to move closer and assess the situation, but I also didn't want to get too close. I didn't want to see Dad lying down looking helpless if that was the extent of it. I wasn't sure what I would do if I saw him like that. I thought of all the times I could have come home and refused his invitations.

As much as I didn't want to be back here, or be part of the new family he'd made, he was still my dad. He was still my family. I might resent his choices, but that wasn't a good enough excuse to not see my old man when he'd requested it of me. Even if it was more of a demand than a request.

But I couldn't picture Matthew Thompson lying down looking all helpless, and I didn't think I could remove the picture from my mind if I did see it.

I didn't get to because as the two paramedics exited the ambulance, my step-mother, Alice came after them. I was surprised to see her there, though why should I? She was the man's wife. My nose scrunched up as I stepped back.

She was the one person I didn't want to see the most. I'd been avoiding thinking about her at all, but with her now in front of me, I couldn't help myself going on the defensive. My back straightened and I forced my face to be expressionless. If there were one person I would never willingly show any emotion to, it was this woman, because if I did it would be intense dislike.

That would just be rude, wouldn't it?

"Hello, Trent," she said, smiling at me. "I'm surprised to see you here. Emily said you were coming back home, but…"

I just stood there, trying very hard not to scowl down at her. She was a small woman, and with my six-foot-five height, I pretty much dwarfed her.

"How've you been?" she asked, and I wondered why she was even trying to strike up a conversation.

She and I had barely talked in all the years we'd lived in the same house. When I couldn't avoid her, she'd start talking to me, and I would either stare at her until she stopped, or I would walk away. There was nothing I had to say to her, anyway. Well, besides one thing.

You stole everything from me.

They were words I'd thought about her since the moment she came into our family. I was sad after my mom's death, but eventually, I would have been fine. Maybe not got over it, but got used to the heartbreak enough that it didn't hurt quite as badly every day.

But then my dad met this woman, and she took his love away from me. The day she walked into the mansion, Dad was all smiles while I was still grieving, and afterward, he spent even less time with me than he had before Mom had died. I'd seen him sitting alone in his office a few times, staring off into nothing, so I thought he was grieving the same as me. I didn't mind that he didn't make time for me because he was hurting as well.

Alice showing up out of nowhere was like a slap in the face.

He didn't wait all that long for her to give him offspring. More distractions away from me. To the point he probably had no idea what was going on with me by the time I hit my teens. So I'd just neglected to tell him I was leaving when it came to college. I just packed my things one day and left, only for him to call me a month later wondering where the hell I'd gone.

A fucking month. That was how long it took my dad to remember I still existed after I left the mansion, and even then, only because my brothers were asking for me.

Just how long would he have ignored my absence, too busy with his new family to notice his eldest son had left the nest?

I had distanced myself from my family, from my dad. But it wasn't like I'd done it all on my own. He didn't reach out to me much, either. He'd forced me to tell him the day of my graduation, only for him to not be there, for both the end of high school and university. Then he'd told me to let him know when I started working so he could help me, only to call again several months later wondering why I didn't ask for his help.

He didn't get it was because I didn't want it. I'd wanted to build things up on my own, and I did. Having his support would have been enough for me. If only the old bastard had had some faith in me instead of trying to run things behind the scenes.

Even though I'd been young when changes started to happen to him, I was always a smart kid, and I understood.

His attention turned to the first baby, then the second, then the third, and there was no room for me. It looked like they didn't need me anymore, so why would I have gone back anyway?

My father had changed, and I attributed all of it to this woman in front of me.

"I just wanted to check on Dad," I said, forcing my voice to be polite. "I'm sorry, I didn't know you would be here. I'll just come back later…"

I tried to look over her shoulder as the paramedics pulled someone out of the ambulance, but she stood firmly in my way. I tried to go around her, only for her to move with me. I felt like I was about to snap, and I glared at the small woman in front of me.

"What are you doing?" I asked. "I need to get into the house too, you know. Unless you want to kick me out now?"

A delicate frown appeared on her forehead. "Trent, I would never try to kick you out of your home."

I snorted, disbelieving. You did it anyway, didn't you? Don't pretend now, step-mother.

"Fine then. Emily wouldn't tell me anything but you must have been with him. Can you tell me what Dad's situation is?"

She didn't speak immediately, her hands coming up to resettle the scarf she had around her neck. She looked uneasy, and it reminded me so much of Emily from before.

I scowled. "What can't you tell me? I've already had Emily dancing around the subject. Don't mess with me, Alice. Tell me what's happening with my father."

She winced as I called her by first name, and I scoffed internally, wondering if she expected me to call her mom or something. So what if she'd known me since I was five? I didn't consider her a replacement for my mother. If anything, I'd always thought of her as an intruder, and even after more than twenty years since we'd met, I wouldn't think any differently.

"Trent," she said hesitantly, looking up to meet my eyes. "I'm afraid that… your father doesn't want to see you."

I blinked down at her, tilting my head slightly to the side. I must have heard her wrong.

"What did you just say?" I asked. "Please repeat it because I think I must have heard you wrong."

"You didn't. Your father refuses to see you, Trent. I'm sorry."

No, I wanted to say. There was no reason why Dad would refuse to see me. He was the one always badgering me to come back, and now that I had he didn't want to see me?

My heart clenched as I thought maybe he was in a really bad state. My father had his pride, after all, and it was even greater than my own. If I didn't want to see my dad lying down all helpless, he wouldn't want his children seeing him that way.

But then, I narrowed my eyes at Alice. "Did you say something to him?"

She looked offended, but I couldn't put it past her.

"Of course not! I swear, Trent, I tried to get him to agree to see you since you finally came home, but he just kept saying no. I'm sorry."

I snorted at her apology. I didn't need one from her for any reason.

"This isn't my home," I told her bluntly, then went to walk around her. She didn't stop me now that Dad must have been taken out of sight. "This hasn't been home for me for a long time."

I ignored how my heart ached as I stomped back into the house.

Just why the fuck did I come back here? I wondered to myself.

My father couldn't be bothered to see me, so why did Emily call me and tell me to come back? I was so fucking annoyed, enough that I could have just gone back to my room, packed my suitcase, and gone back into my car. I was so tempted to drive back to my own life, where everything wasn't so complicated or annoying.

Work was stressful, but compared to dealing with my family it was a walk in the park.

But even if he didn't want to see me there was still work to be done. And besides, I'd left things unfinished at my office. I could use some time to finish things up instead of wasting more time on this trip. I'd arrived barely an hour ago, and even with all the stops I'd made, I felt exhausted.

I just wouldn't let it show.

I made my way to my father's office and phoned my PA to let her know I would be working remotely for a while until things settled enough that me being out of the office wouldn't bring things crashing down. I needed to protect the life I'd built, make sure it was still there when I went back to it.

Because of course, I would be going back. I wasn't wanted around here, I never had been. The moment I got any news about Dad I'd pack up and leave again, likely for the last time.

6

JESSI

The sun was just peeking over the horizon when I glanced through a window after I arrived at the hotel. I didn't have anything to do yet, so I was lounging in the staff area out of uniform before my shift started in an hour or so. I was drinking a cup of mocha I'd made myself, with extra chocolate, cream, and sugar, and some whipped cream and marshmallows sprinkled on top. I lightly stirred it before eating some of the whipped cream and marsh-mallow combo, and then drank some of the mocha as I stared off into space, my thoughts only a few miles away. If the level of whipped cream went down, I'd add some more without thinking, I was enjoying the treat but my mind was a whirlwind.

I was spraying on some more whipped cream when the door to the staff room opened, causing me to look up and accidentally spray more than I'd wanted to.

It was Laura, and she arched an expertly shaped blond eyebrow at me and then at the mug in my hand.

"Are you drowning your sorrows in sugar, Jessi? Because that's more likely to give you diabetes than anything," she said, tilting her head at the mug. Her long hair was pulled into a tight ponytail and for a moment it looked like a squirrel dancing on her shoulder. I had to hold back a snort of laughter as she tilted her head the other way quizzically.

I looked down and winced when I saw what was inside my mug. The mocha was about halfway gone, but the whipped cream overflowed the cup.

"More like gain weight," I muttered, sighing as I licked it. "I do watch my sugar intake with all the pastries I make, I'm just giving myself a desperately needed treat today."

I stared at my drink, wondering if this wasn't a little too much of a treat. I did try to keep fit. My body had grown shapelier as I grew out of puberty and my teens, but I didn't always picture it as a good thing. I didn't brag about it, but I was a little buxom. As a late-bloomer, I didn't really grow out until after high school, when I started turning quite a few heads. It had helped slightly with my self-esteem. But only slightly, because being ogled wasn't something I enjoyed, especially when most men's eyes fell to my chest instead of looking at my face when I talked to them.

That was only one of the annoying things.

Having a slightly big chest sometimes got in the way of my work. I'd grown used to it, so it no longer got in my way but getting used to the changes in my body had taken me a long time, and sometimes it still annoyed me. I would have rather been slightly smaller, but I couldn't change the way my body was.

The other thing was my wide hips and my ass. Not to mention all those meals that went to my middle, my thighs, and my hips. It caused me to exercise more than I would have liked, because I was one of those lazy girls in high school that would run a few feet then pause, doubled over, feeling like I was about to pass out and breathing like I'd run a mile.

I needed the exercise, though. I was just a little conscious of my weight and shape.

"If you're not gonna finish it, can I have it instead?" Laura asked with a hopeful gleam in her eyes.

"Was that the real reason behind your questioning? You just wanted to have it for yourself?"

"I have a feeling you're drinking a mocha, and yours are always the best. Make me one?"

I shook my head, and she sighed again.

Laura crossed the room to the kitchen area of the staff room. We didn't eat the same food we made for the guests, more often than not having to make our separate meals. The hotel was awesome in that the kitchen in the staff room was about as well equipped as the kitchen we used to cater to the guests, if a little smaller. Laura got herself a cup of coffee, then came to where I sat in the lounge area and took the couch across from me.

"So," she started after she'd taken a sip, then held the cup between her hands, looking up at me expectantly. "Do I get to hear why you're drowning yourself in sugar this early in the morning and won't share in the hedonism? Something happened?"

I sighed, not really wanting to get into it, but last night was still plaguing me.

Laura and I weren't just colleagues; we were also friends. I wouldn't call us so close that I'd told her all the sordid details of my life and how it tied in with the Thompson family. But she was such a nice, happy person that she got along with pretty much anybody and every-body. She worked as a maid and I worked in the kitchens, so we didn't get to meet all that often, unless we both happened to be in the staffroom at the same time, or if she came looking for me.

After a moment of thinking about it, I figured there was nothing wrong with telling her. She rarely gossiped, so I knew I could trust her.

I took a sip of my mocha, chewed on a slightly soggy marshmallow, then looked over at her.

"I saw Trent Thompson," I admitted. "You know my mom works over at their place, right? Well, I ran into him yesterday." Literally.

She tilted her head slightly to the side, confused for a moment before her eyes widened in realization. I wasn't sure whether I wanted to laugh at her expression or her dancing squirrel more. I breathed my laughter out and waited for her response.

"Oh! The one you have a history with, right? I've only ever heard of him, I've never had the chance as to even see him. He's the oldest, right?"

"How do you even know about that? I don't think I've ever mentioned it to you…"

She had the grace to look sheepish. "Well, I hear things

around. And the rumor mills have been going wild around here the moment people heard the Thompson sons would be coming back."

I frowned. "I don't think there are people who know that he and I have history, though…"

She arched an eyebrow at me. "You do realize there are people here you probably went to the same high school with or something? They could just be making rumors for the fun of it, but I'm pretty good at distinguishing what's true and what's not." She grinned. "Like, there's one that says the two of you had an affair in his last year of high school, so his dad sent him away to keep the two of you apart, and you sticking around here for work is the reason why he's never been back."

I snorted at the ridiculousness of it. "Trent isn't the kind of person who would just do whatever he was told. I'm pretty sure he left on his own because he wanted to. And there was no affair." I grimaced. "I told him I liked him and he laughed in my face," I admitted, my voice quietly shaking.

Laura's eyes widened again. "Wow," she breathed. "Fuck, that's bad. Seeing him again can't be easy for you, can it?"

"It's not. Not at all. What I want to do is avoid him, but that means never going to visit my mom, and she's going to ask me why."

The expression in her eyes was sympathetic. "She doesn't know that you had a crush on him and got heartbroken?"

More like I *still* had a crush on him. And it broke my

heart every day. Especially with him around and acting like an asshole. My silence pretty much told her everything.

"You wanna know what I'm dreading? Mason," she said with a wrinkle of her nose.

I sent her a grateful look for changing the subject for my sake.

"Why?" I asked. Mason was the middle brother of the Thompson clan. He was a few years younger than me, not quite as young as Emily, but I'd never really talked to him before.

Laura shot me a part-incredulous, part-horrified look. "How could you even ask that! He comes around here a lot, you know? I'm dreading him getting back here because that guy always throws wild parties. Do you know how hard it is cleaning up after him? It's a freaking nightmare for all us maids. I'm not the only one a little more than sick of it."

I felt my face twist into disgust. "That bad is it?"

She nodded quickly. "You don't get to see a lot of it because he never asks for dessert for any of his parties, just food sometimes, and there'll always be plenty of alcohol." She narrowed her eyes slyly at me. "Hey, why don't we put our heads together and see what we can do about our problems with these Thompson boys, huh?"

"It's not like we can touch them. They might as well be our bosses."

Laura rolled her eyes. "That's not what I meant. I thought we could get away from it for a while and badmouth them behind their backs. You probably need it, and I know I do. We could make it into a girls' night out."

When she put it like that, I became interested. She was right; I had quite a few things to do with Trent that I would love to get out with someone I trusted. Emily and I were friends too, but even though she wasn't close with her brother, it was awkward for me to talk to her about it. Laura's plan sounded perfect.

"I guess we could set something like that up," I said, then finished my mocha. "When do you think we should go?"

Laura was suddenly full of enthusiasm. She leaned forward, eyes wide open and practically sparkling as she opened her mouth to speak.

Only, she never got the chance to. She was interrupted when the door opened, and I looked up, my face going blank with shock when I saw the last person I would have expected to see.

Trent.

"What are you doing here?" I blurted, more out of surprise than really demanding to know.

He stuck his hands in the pockets of his slacks and arched a condescending eyebrow at me. Nobody with blond eyebrows should be able to look that condescending, I thought, just before he spoke and destroyed my day. Again.

"Shouldn't I be asking you that? What are you doing at the hotel? Or are you still trying to follow me everywhere?"

I was too shocked for a moment to even respond. What was Trent doing in the staff area? It was the one place I'd thought I would never have to see him! I'd thought I'd be safe there. But then his words registered, and I narrowed my eyes at him.

"Not everything in my life is about you, you know," I retorted. "I'm here because I work here now. My shift is about to start. I work in the kitchen."

There was a minute show of surprise on his face, and I would have missed it if I wasn't looking at him so intently. But I caught the slight twitch of his eyebrows and felt a little smug that he didn't have an immediate response.

That didn't last long though.

"What did you do?" he asked with a sneer. "Because you did something, right? Or did someone owe you a huge favor, and that's how you landed a job here as a chef?"

I stared at him with my jaw dropped. With the way he was looking at me up and down, I had a good idea what he was thinking. As if I would ever stoop to something so low! In spite of the fact that seeing him in front of me was making my heart beat out of control, there was no way I was going to take shit from this guy after all the crap he'd already given me over the years.

"Excuse you, Trent," I growled, scowling at him as I tilted my chin up. "But I got my job here because I worked my ass off, meaning I got it the old-fashioned way."

He smirked, but I wasn't quite done yet.

"I know you like to look down on me," I continued, narrowing my eyes at his look, "but believe it or not, I managed to get to school and worked my ass off to get through. I got a scholarship and several jobs even to manage. We're not all like some people who can buy their way through a university education. I finished school, applied for a job, and worked from the bottom of the hotel to get to where I'm at right now."

He'd lost the smirk, and I couldn't help but flash a look of triumph.

"Just how good can you be?" he said with a scoff.

"You know the standards your dad has," I returned. "Especially for this hotel, since it's the closest one to home. I've done a good enough job that he met me personally and offered me a job at any of the other hotel branches around the world. The only reason I stuck around here was because I didn't want to move too far away from my parents."

I didn't know what I expected from Trent exactly. It wasn't like he was going to pat me on the head and tell me I'd done a good job. It would be condescending, but I probably would have been happy. Him looking at me a little differently would have been enough for me as well. Hell, I would have settled for him ignoring me and just leaving.

But the way he looked at me, it was with the same ridicule from over a decade ago. Suddenly, under his gaze, I was that same gangly teenager having my dreams stomped into the ground by the boy of my dreams. I could feel my cheeks start to flame in embarrassment, and I hated how he could still affect me with just a look even after all this time.

He can't be thinking about it, I thought frantically. But he was looking me up and down with the same derision, and I knew he was. My mind went back all those years to when I'd kissed him and confessed my feelings for him. Trent was thinking about that kiss, the second most embarrassing thing that had happened to me that day besides him laughing at me afterward.

Why am I not saying anything?

I had a lot to say to him about that day. If he was going to give me looks like the one he was giving me, I at least wanted to let him know what an ass he'd been, and how I'd disliked him since that day. It would be a lie, and he probably wouldn't care. It might not even make me feel better. But I wanted to say the words, if only to find some closure and finally move on from this man.

But I just stood in front of him, my body starting to tremble the longer he just stood there staring at me. Like he knew how he was affecting me, he smirked again. He didn't even say anything, just turned around and walked away. I watched his back until he was out of sight.

"Wow."

I turned to Laura, who'd been sitting there silently the whole time and all but ignored. It had felt like there was only Trent and me in the room, and I felt my face grow even hotter.

"That man is a piece of work."

I just growled. I'd jumped to my feet at some point as I defended myself against him, and I let out an explosive sigh as I plopped back into it. My body was still trembling, and I could feel the sting of frustrated tears in my eyes. I refused to let them fall. I wouldn't cry again for a guy like that.

"I just want to strangle him!" I growled to myself as much as to Laura, my fingers clenching into fists at my side as I tried to control my emotions. "Maybe if I cut off some of the air into his brain he might become a little less of a bastard."

Not that I ever would. It would mean touching him, and even as irritated as I felt, I knew I'd be doing something other than strangling his neck if I ever got my hands on him again.

Like she knew the route my thoughts were taking, Laura gave me a strange look. She didn't say anything out loud, and I was grateful.

7

———

TRENT

I turned my back to Jessi and walked away, it was the last thing I wanted to do, but seeing her like that, there was no way I could have stayed and kept my composure. My smirk fell away and changed into a look of relief once I was out of their sight.

That was too close.

I was impressed that she'd had the courage to speak up to me when she'd usually just cowed or ran away before. It had taken all I had not to let my eyes drop to her luscious body. I vividly remembered feeling her pressed up against me, even for that short moment when she'd run into me. I'd wanted to close the space between us, reach for her and hold her to me again, only longer.

Shit.

"Don't lose your head now, Trent," I said to myself, pausing when a maid walked past me with a giggle.

I'd slowed down without realizing it, then speed-walked out of there with my chin held high.

Why had I even bothered to go to the staff area? I was taking over the higher management of the hotel, but I could always leave the little things to the hotel manager. My meticulous nature just wouldn't let me. I hadn't gotten as far as I had in my career by letting other people do jobs for me.

When can I go back to that again? I thought wistfully about the past, and how I just wanted to get back to my own business as quickly as possible.

Then I remembered what Jessi looked like as she told me off: her blonde-brown hair was tied back in a ponytail with wisps falling around her face, her cheeks were lit up a light-pink, and there'd been this small furrow in her brow as she scowled at me. I, of course, found the picture completely endearing because I was a masochist.

Don't even think about it!

I growled the thought silently to myself, feeling more relaxed as I walked into the elevator for it to take me up. "She is not the woman for you. You decided that long before you left."

I hadn't been nice about it either.

No matter how rude I'd been to her—was still being, in fact—I'd always liked her. Back before I left, when I was dealing with a lot of family shit, she would always seem to be there when I turned around, no matter how much I kept telling her to leave me alone. Something about her just bugged me.

Her sweet eyes... Her light-brown eyes that always looked at me with so much understanding made me uncomfortable as a teenager when I was more than ready to push away anything and everything in my hurry to get away. Even before she confessed that she wanted me just as much as I wanted her. It wasn't a surprise. I'd known, just from the look in her eye. It had always made me uncomfortable that she might expect something like that from me.

I knew I wasn't the loving kind, so when she finally plucked some courage and told me, I had been cruel to her to get her to stop. Fucking, definitely, but loving? I didn't believe in that shit, and I'd known I couldn't give her what she wanted.

Love only ever ended badly as far as I'd seen or cared. I had a dad who was absent more often than not and yet complained that I wasn't there for the family, one I wanted no part of. There was my stepmother, who I couldn't stand, yet was so eager to please Dad that she'd try to get along with me even as I rebuffed her. I'd known the moment Dad brought her home I wasn't going to give her a chance to be my stepmother, but that fact didn't matter.

I hated her, and that was it. There was no reason to think it over; no matter how many times both of them insisted I did.

"Stop being such an arrogant pig!"

The whole thing was driving me fucking insane. I was having conversations with myself in public, and I didn't even realize it as the elevator doors opened.

"I'm sorry?"

The woman who worked as my dad's secretary stood on the other side with a shocked expression on her face. I quickly cleared my throat and to stop her thinking that I'd gone insane, I changed the subject.

"Is there any news from my father?" I asked, stepping out of the elevator, and she fell into step beside me as I headed for the office.

"Not yet, sir. He's still refusing to see you."

I frowned because it wasn't what I wanted to hear. I was hoping that there'd been some change, but it was clear that there was none.

"Did you at least get a reason as to why?"

She shook her head. "I'm sorry. Were you talking to me?"

Fuck!

I need to get my thoughts back to the business and nothing else. Otherwise, I will go fucking insane.

"Forget it," I said. "Tell me how things are going and if there's something I need to do that Dad was supposed to be doing."

I grumbled to myself silently as she started listing things out beside me and I listened with half an ear. What exactly was the old man planning?

Would Dad continue to refuse to see me until I got so impatient I just knocked his door down? He was lucky I didn't pack up and go home. If he didn't want to see me, what reason did I have to stick around?

But the truth was that he wouldn't be in the office, and my stepmother could hardly handle those affairs. Supposedly all my brothers had been called, but I arrived first because I was the closest, and the other two were yet to get there. I couldn't just leave the handling of the hotel to the secretary, so took it upon myself to handle my dad's affairs, or I wouldn't have been at the hotel at all.

By the time we got to the office, she finished giving me the run down. I listened half-heartedly, my thoughts of the girl from the past now on my mind. I needed to stop thinking about my cock and just my head; there was too much at stake to get distracted by Jessi. I rounded the desk, took off my jacket and draped it on the back of the chair before sitting down. Then I looked back up at my secretary.

"Put off my dad's meetings for the next couple of days. If he doesn't improve by then, I'll see what I can do about it." I couldn't just go into his meetings without preparation. I knew my dad, and if I blew things for his precious hotel—though I was confident enough in my abilities to know I wouldn't, it didn't hurt to be cautious—he'd make me pay for it. "I'll need some paperwork from the manager, so call him and ask him to bring them up. Where can I find everything else I need to take care of?"

"I'll bring the files over to you and call the manager," she said, making an about turn and marching out of the room without another word or quibble.

One thing about Dad was he had good taste, that was for sure. One wouldn't be blamed for thinking Dad hired his secretary based on her looks and nothing else. This one was different, she was efficient, which was more than could be said for the others.

I tried to work and looked over contracts with business partners and sheets with hotel costs, but the interlude with Jessi this morning just wouldn't leave my mind.

I could try to deny it to myself, but she had really got to me with her defiant beauty and courage. She gave me just as much venom as I'd given her at the same time, and it turned out it was a combo guaranteed to make my blood heat up. I'd shake my head every now and then to try to focus, only I'd remember the way she glared at me all over again. In another hour, I hadn't done much, and I was a little hard in my slacks. I groaned to myself and wondered if I'd been alone too long. When was the last time a woman graced my bed?

But as I tried to imagine the kind of women I usually brought home for a little fun, Jessi's image wouldn't leave me alone. Instead, I thought back to when she'd been a teenager, one of the last times I'd seen her before I left town.

Even back when she'd been all gangly, clumsy and awkward, there would be times when I would find myself looking at her. I remembered the kiss she gave me. I hadn't been able to forget it for months, and it took finding a multitude of girls to distract me before I was sure I'd put her behind me, only sparing the occasional thought for Jessi over the years.

But that kiss, I remembered it. I'd kissed and been kissed before, sure, but something about the way she did it, so soft and sweetly, followed by a confession, had thrown me for a moment. It had started this longing in me for everything I'd lost when Mom died, made me want so much more from life than money and women on my arm as temporary distractions from life, because even as a teenager I'd done that. If Jessi had known just how many girls had kissed me before she did, she might have thought twice about it.

She didn't though, and I had an annoying memory to deal with for the rest of my life because I'd known my longing was only foolish. What I'd needed in my life was the ability to lead it on my own, how I wanted to. I'd pushed Jessi away, laughed in her face to make her run from me because I knew I couldn't have a woman like her. Things would just end terribly for the both of us.

The starlets, models, and socialites that I went out with in public and occasionally warmed my bed, then left without complaint or trying to be clingy, were the most I deserved as far as companionship went. I couldn't treat a sweet woman right, and the women I went for were never hurt by how I treated them. I wasn't disrespectful, but it was rare I ever called them back. We'd meet at some big party later with someone else on my arm, and none of them would bat an eyelash.

Maybe I should call one of them here, I thought to myself.

But I hadn't seen anyone in three weeks because I'd been busy at work. I may not be doing my job at the moment, but that was still true. Besides not having the time for it, it was the wrong time even to be thinking of romance with my dad being ill.

"Even if that old man refuses to see me," I growled.

A knock on the door made me look up. I thought it might be the secretary, or someone from the hotel coming to ask about something important, but the door opened without me calling for it too, and my brother Mason walked in.

"When did you get here?" I asked in not quite a greeting.

He grinned, pulling off his shades. "About an hour ago. I stopped by the house but there was no news, and Emily let me know you'd be here."

Mason looked like his usual self, though it had been a few months since I'd seen him last. But then, he never really changed, did he?

He was shorter than me by an inch at six foot four, and I stood up as he crossed the room to keep him aware of that fact. We had the same gray eyes, but his blonde hair was a few shades darker than mine. He reached a hand across the desk as he stopped on the other side of it, and after a short hesitation he probably didn't catch, I shook his hand. Then we both sat down.

"So?" he started saying, and I was already growing impatient, hoping he would just say what was on his mind. "What exactly is going on? I get an urgent call from Emily that Dad had a heart attack, only she seems more nervous than worried and won't tell me anything about him. Even Mom isn't saying anything."

"Are you still trying to talk to your mom?" I asked because I knew I wouldn't dare do that. It would mean having to acknowledge her existence, and I tried not to do that as much as possible. "She came back with him in an ambulance yesterday when he should probably still be in the hospital. That man is far too stubborn for his own good! Always thinking he's Superman or something."

He sighed and tipped his head back. "I tried insisting, but Mom's just like that. If she doesn't want to say something, you can't talk her into it, not even her kids." He raised his head to look at me with an uncharacteristic frown. He was the always ready to party one, so seeing him so serious was nice for a change. "You don't think it's really serious, do you? He's practically retired, though that just means he works here instead of looking into all the branches because he's not the kind to stay at home idle. It's probably bad that he's not here working, isn't it?"

I frowned as I arranged my thoughts. They were along the same lines as his. We all knew what our dad was like, after all.

"It probably is something serious," I said slowly. "And he just calls himself retired, but I know he never stopped working." He just asked me to take care of some of the other hotels and left other managers in charge of what I wasn't taking care off, adding more to my plate without asking me if I even wanted a hand in his empire. "He's refused to see me, so I guess we just have to wait until he stops being so damn shy."

Mason snorted. "Since when was that shameless old man shy?"

I rolled my eyes as he chuckled. "Anyway, while he's off, there's a lot of work to do at the hotel. I'll be looking into the other branches in a few days if we still have no news, but there's plenty to get done here that he left behind."

Mason's expression went serious again as he leaned forward, elbows braced on the arms of the chair and hands linked together over his lap.

"Tell me what there is and I'll see what I can help you with."

I gave him a suspicious look. He waved my expression away, looking amused. "Dad taught all of us about the business, not just you, you know." He waited for my reaction, but I didn't give him one so he just carried on talking. "I can be of some help. Or if you want, I could leave it all in your capable hands, big bro." He gave me a strange look. "Though I was kinda surprised to hear you were in the area, Trent. I didn't believe it, which is why I rushed to get here just to see it for myself."

"Forget that. Focus on work for now. You might as well make yourself useful while you're here."

I showed him the same list the secretary had given me. We divided some duties between us, everyone with their shit to take care of, just as our dad taught us.

Though I'd acted all skeptical about his offer considering what he liked to do with his free time, I wouldn't doubt his capabilities. Our dad had been a hard man after all, especially when it came to the business. But he taught us, even the other four—Emily too, though she was the least interested—how to be proper businessmen, at least.

"But first," I told him before he could get his ass out of the chair, "I need help with some of the paperwork right now, or I'll be lost in it for the rest of the day, and I have other stuff I want to get done today."

He arched an eyebrow at the papers I already had in front of me, and the thick pile of folders to the side that I'd yet to get to.

"Just how much is there, anyway?" he asked, part curious and partly horrified.

I shrugged. "It must have all been waiting for a week, at least. Maybe he wasn't feeling well before the heart attack, or he would have done it all himself."

"Yeah," he said with a frown as we shared a worried glance. "I've never heard of him taking a day off work for anything short of a broken arm. And even then he still shows up."

I didn't answer. I was trying not to think too hard or too much about what was going on with our dad, or I'd worry myself to death. Mason didn't say anything either and we got down to business.

Now, I thought to myself, once Mason was looking over some of the paperwork, if only I could get Jessi out of my mind.

But I knew it would be a futile effort even to try, and I was annoyed at myself for it.

8

―――

JESSI

*W*hy am I still thinking about that bastard?

I was in the middle of my shift, finishing dessert after dessert for the guests. I wasn't my usual efficient self because that bastard was still in my head even hours later. I found myself making mistakes. They were little mistakes, not the kind of things just anyone could notice, but a few of my fellow cooks were shooting me curious looks.

Fuck. I couldn't get the attention of the head chef. I couldn't stand that guy most days because he was so damn bossy.

"Jessi?"

"Hm?" I whirled around when someone called my name, to find one of the servers standing awkwardly to the side.

"Um, I'm waiting for the strawberry shortcake slices? Are you done?"

"Oh!" I looked back to where I was still decorating

them. "I'm so sorry! I thought I finished already. Just give me a quick minute!"

I didn't know whether he would take the lie, but he stood silently as I finished decorating. It came out pretty good, but I still winced as I watched them get carried away. I was my own worst critic, even when I got praise. The taste would be good, but it was also supposed to look good, and while that quick job made it look okay, it was not my usual best.

"You've got to get it together," I told myself, taking in a deep breath, then letting it out. "Calm, completely calm, think about nothing but work…"

I was so focused trying to calm my thoughts, I didn't notice when someone else walked up to me.

"Jessi?"

For the second time, I was startled into whirling around. Mark was standing in front of me.

"Do I have another order?"

"Yeah," he said slowly, giving me a strange look as he handed over the slip. "Are you okay, though? Because you're distracted today, and if it's going to be a problem and you need some help…?"

"No, no," I jumped in quickly, waving my hands. "It's nothing, just feeling a little tired because I didn't get enough sleep last night." Well, it was true. I could barely sleep because all I could think about was Trent, and how much I hadn't wanted to run into him again. It had happened anyway. "I promise I'm good to work, so don't worry."

"Okay," he said, then shrugged and turned to go back to his area, shooting a last look at me.

Now that I was paying attention to the people in the room, I realized a lot of them kept shooting me looks. They were all probably worried because I wasn't acting like myself. Ever since I'd started working there, I'd never been anything but professional. But then there'd never been any personal feelings to get in the way of work before.

I wish I could talk to Laura right now, I thought to myself wistfully, but it would have to wait.

I hadn't told her much about what went down between Trent and me, back then or recently, but I'd told her enough. Plus, Laura had listened to our whole exchange earlier which meant I had to tell her a bit more to explain.

Now she knew about my embarrassing crush. The one that a lot of my friends back in high school had known about, but they'd all feigned ignorance to protect my pride. I was pretty sure they realized when I got rejected, too, but then I stopped talking to them after that—so few as they were—and isolated myself for the following few years as I worked hard through school for the sake of landing a scholarship.

"We're going out tonight," had been Laura's deciding words. "I thought we could set the plan for a few days later, or maybe in a couple of weeks, but after all that, you're going to need something tonight."

I'd listened to her declaration because she added we would need good tiramisu—that we would be making ourselves—to make a proper evening of it. It was one of my favorite desserts, so I was all for it.

I had a lot of work to do, and nothing else should be on my mind, I reminded myself. Nothing!

"Jessi! We've got more orders, so move it, will you?" I heard from behind me somewhere and gave a wave of acknowledgment.

"Sorry!" I called out an apology, taking the next slip of paper.

Normally, the menu would be planned, and I had about thirty percent option in the planning. My menu changed every few days to add or remove certain pastries or desserts, though there were some that always remained because they were old favorites and always sold out. I knew there could be lots of orders and it would be too ridiculous to try and bake a cake when they were asked for, so I had several different types of cakes baked from earlier in the morning once I started my shift.

The day passed by slowly for me after the lunch service, which always happened when the only thing that I wanted it to do was to go by quickly, so I didn't get distracted again. By the time I'd finished making all the dessert orders for the evening, I was worn out. Everyone else cleared out of the kitchens, leaving me alone.

Laura found me lying down on a couch in the staff room twenty minutes later.

"Tired?" she guessed, then let out a loud sigh. "Me too. No, I'm exhausted. Tired is just a small way to describe how I feel at the moment and I felt even worse when I heard the good news."

I arched an eyebrow at her.

"What good news?" I asked.

She smiled brightly, her voice sounding fake when she brightly exclaimed. "Mason's plane landed today! He's also at the hotel, right at this very moment!"

"I didn't hear that," I said, frowning.

She sighed, plopping down across from me again, fake bright expression dropping. "That's because he hasn't started making demands or making a mess yet. I heard he came to the hotel and went right up to the office."

She stopped and looked at me with a deep frown, but I didn't need her to finish her sentence. He must have gone to where Trent was.

"Well," I said, jumping off the couch, suddenly energetic. "Do you want to start cooking here or in the kitchens? I even bought extra ingredients, so we won't have to use anything of the hotel's."

I headed over to the small staff room kitchen, and Laura followed behind me.

"I thought we'd be doing this at your place," she admitted.

I sighed. "Yeah, but my quarters are a bit too small to cook in. I usually just eat all my meals here or go to my mom's."

"Over at the mansion?"

I nodded. "And I won't be going back there for a while."

Hopefully, there would be no more accidental run-ins with Trent in the hotel, and I could survive his trip without seeing his face one more time.

"So how are we doing this?" Laura asked as I set up the ingredients on the counter. "I cook some, but I don't bake, so you're going to have to teach me."

"That's fine. We'll go together. I have this recipe that I love off the top of my head, so I'll just give you directions, and you can help me. Is that okay?"

She grinned at me with growing excitement. "Definitely!"

We started, me calling out for Laura to measure ingredients and hand them over to me as I mixed the batter, then left it to her as I went around setting the oven to preheat, and preparing the tray that would go in. I went back to layer the cake, and between the two of us, the preparation was done in no time, and I was sliding it into the oven.

"That was surprisingly easy," Laura said, watching the oven's glass window.

"Baking is pretty easy when you get used to it, actually, so it's no surprise. I've been doing it with my mom since I was a kid."

She hummed. "I never really did much with my mom growing up. Except maybe argue."

I frowned at her. "Do you guys not get along? Is that why you don't tell me about your family?"

"No, I don't talk about them because there's nothing to talk about. I'm not as close to them as you are with yours, but we're okay."

I looked after the baking cake as she went around the kitchen, looking for a couple of long glasses, then finding where the wine bottles were stashed.

"What do you think would go best with this?" she asked.

It made sense she would ask me, as the chef and all, and I went over to see the selection. I picked a light red, a sweet wine that would just be perfectly coupled with the dessert. No one would mind seeing it missing as long as I replaced it, as was the silent rule with all the staff.

Once the cake was ready to be decorated, I had to be the one to do it. Laura just stood to the side and watched as I started to work my magic on the food; it wasn't so much about the taste of the cake, but all about the presentation. Something I prided myself on doing well. When I'd layered the cake with the filling we moved back over to the couch and sat down, cake and wine settled on the coffee table in front of us.

"Now, where were we?" Laura asked, looking at me as she took a sip from her glass.

I sighed. "We're eating cake, not talking about Trent. The last thing I want to do is talk about him right now."

She nodded in understanding. "You know you can talk to me anytime though, right? And Emily too."

I snorted. "No way. I know him way better than she does, but she's still his sister, you know? It would be awkward."

"I suppose," she admitted, her expression thoughtful. "Though she's a good enough friend if you wanted to badmouth her brother in front of her, she'd probably just join you."

I didn't argue with that. I missed Emily, but she hadn't shown up at the hotel, and I wasn't going back to the mansion now. And I imagined she must have been busy with her Dad being ill. I didn't know if Laura knew that part of the rumors yet, but I didn't mention it just in case. It wasn't my story to tell.

We spent our time gossiping and eating the tiramisu, quickly going through the wine. By the time the bottle was empty, we were just starting to enjoy ourselves, so Laura picked another random bottle and opened it. Time was passing but it didn't matter. I didn't have the early shift in the morning.

After what felt like hours, we were finally getting exhausted and leaned against each other on the couch. I drank the last of my wine and reached over to set my glass on the table, nearly falling over in the process. Laura caught me, saving the glass from slamming into the coffee table with my forearm. I winced at the light ache, then we both dissolved into girlish giggles.

Laura sighed. "Oh, this was fun. I don't know why we didn't try it earlier."

I smiled wryly. "If we did this often our jobs might be in jeopardy. And do you know how much that wine we drank costs? If it hadn't tasted so good, I'd be crying over my bank account right now."

"Really?" she asked, looking at me with a wince. "Do you need me to help you pay for it?"

I waved her off. "Nah, it's fine. I'll handle it tomorrow. Hopefully, no one will need those two bottles for anything."

She let out another sigh. "It's getting pretty late. I should probably be getting home now…"

"Call for a taxi before you step outside," I said in warning. "The area is pretty safe, but it's better to be cautious."

She nodded as she took her phone from her purse and dialed for one. I waited for her until the taxi came, and we parted with a hug, her going to take her taxi, me heading up the stairs to my room.

I was a little tipsy on the steps, and the heaviness of my shoes didn't help. I didn't let myself drink all that often, especially since my parents didn't like it and only took the occasional champagne or wine during a party at the mansion themselves. But I'd already tried the elevator, and I was just tipsy enough that it seemed I couldn't get it to work.

Maybe it's broken, I thought, as I started up the first set of stairs.

I lived several floors up in a room tucked away from the guests' rooms. It was exhausting, climbing up all those steps, and I kept stopping to take a breath and going so slow it took me ten times longer than it would have taken if I'd just gone for the elevator. I could have gone for the one in the lobby used by the guests, but it was a rule that the staff and hotel guests mixed as little as possible outside of duties.

"Finally," I muttered to myself after clearing another set of stairs, to realize I'd made it to my floor.

I pulled the door to exit the stairs, stumped for a moment when it wouldn't open. Then I remembered I was supposed to push it, so I did. Only I pushed with too much force and went barreling out—right into the wide chest of the one person I didn't want to see at that moment.

Trent.

"Hey, there," he said, catching me as I fell into him, and looking at me with a frown. "Do you ever watch where you're going, Jessi?"

But I was hardly paying attention to his words, because for the first time since he'd got back, I was looking at him and not trying to find the teenage kid I'd known in the grown man's face.

"Trent," I murmured more to myself than him. "Fancy meeting you here."

He frowned harder, but I was hardly paying attention to his bad mood.

It was like looking at him for the first time, as though I hadn't really seen the man Trent had become before. I hadn't noticed, but he had changed. Just like me. He'd been a high school boy before, closer to the end of puberty than I was. Being this close to him again and looking at him now, I could see those changes.

In the swift brutal moments I'd seen him before, I hadn't had time to notice that his shoulders had broadened, and he must either be the outdoors type or go to the gym a lot because the muscles I could feel under my hands beneath his suit coat were very well developed. Enough that I had to swallow back spit because I was just chomping at the bit to see.

When did I even put my hands on him? When did I land on him?

He'd been muscled when he was younger, but had he been this big? He might have gained a couple of inches to reach his current six foot five, though it could just be my mind highlighting how delectable he was now than when he'd been an arrogant little boy making me miserable.

I was different from the girl I'd been back then, too. I was a woman now, and my body lit up with our proximity as if to remind me of it. I gasped as my body began to grow warm, especially burning where he had his hands on the small of my back, thumbs digging a little into my waist.

Our bodies were pressed together, and I could feel my nipples harden under my clothes, aching where we were pressed together. And when I squirmed, it sent pleasure curling in my abdomen, making my body tremble.

"Why does your breath smell so sweet?" Trent suddenly asked, the look on his face changing.

I couldn't say anything in return, because all I could think was how handsome he was, with his light gray eyes and blond hair with a gold tint. How beautifully hurt he looked every time I saw him, even when he was putting up a front for everyone else. I was the one who'd seen him in the times when he'd allowed himself to look vulnerable. I knew he wasn't the type to just forget his pain. Even after all these years, he would carry it with him.

All those thoughts swirling through my head were what kept me so preoccupied that I didn't even try to pull away from his arms.

"Sorry," I whispered. "I drunk a little wine with my dessert." Though it was more like a lot. Sharing two bottles of wine between two people…

"Were you just out?" he asked, his voice quiet, almost distracted as he watched my lips and eyes.

I wondered why he wasn't pushing me away.

"Um, no." I tilted my head toward the stairs. "I was just in the staff room with a friend, but she doesn't stay here like I do."

"You're not slurring. But I guess you did fall on me," he

said with a quirk on his lips.

I pouted, but I didn't miss that this was the nicest he'd been to me in years. Not since we were kids.

As if he suddenly seemed to realize, he caught himself and went to pull away from me. I wasn't having it, though. I hadn't been this close to him before, close enough to catch the scent of his cologne and feel his breath on my face. My body moved instinctively on its own, my arms circling his throat and holding him close as I rose up on the tips of my toes, eyes sliding closed as I slid my mouth over his.

There go my inhibitions, I thought, not caring. I'd wanted this for so long, since the first time I'd kissed him, and I was just tipsy enough to have the courage not to back away from what I wanted when I'd finally had him caught off guard.

Trent let out a gasp, and I took advantage. I slid my tongue through his parted lips and explored the inside of his mouth, tentatively at first. His body had gone still against mine, but I didn't stop, coaxing him into the kiss until he hesitantly kissed me back. With both of us participating, the kiss quickly grew in passion, and I found myself clinging to him and panting as our lips parted and met in kiss after kiss.

"Fuck," Trent growled, his breathing ragged when he finally pulled away. "We're out in the damn hallway."

I didn't care. My eyes were closed, my thoughts still muddled from his latest kiss, and I was already leaning in for more. He didn't push me away, accepting the kiss.

Then abruptly, with another curse, he shoved me off

him. I blinked up at him, feeling a little unbalanced on my heels. He kept one hand on my arm and dragged me behind him as we went down the hallway.

"I can't believe I'm fucking doing this," I heard Trent mutter under his breath.

I felt a moment of clarity, wondering just what I was doing too. Trent seemed all for it, but the plan had been to stay away from him, right? I should have left him alone and continued to my room. If he'd been the same asshole from this morning, I would have.

But then he had the door open and he was pulling me inside, turning on the lights and shoving me up against the door, his body following to brace me against it.

"Trent!" I gasped, my breathing picking up again.

He pressed himself fully against me again, and this time I could feel the obvious bulge against my hip. Before I could say anything, his lips were slanted over mine and he was kissing me again. My hands clutched onto his biceps as I squirmed against him, wanting so much more. Whimpers, gasps, and moans fell out of my mouth between the kisses, and he didn't stop until I was almost passing out from lack of breath.

"Jessi," Trent whispered, and the way he said my name had me taking a sharp breath, my body shivering. "I want you, Jessi. So badly. Right now."

His admission was the last straw for me. All thoughts of holding back disappeared, and my hands reached for his clothes. We scrambled to strip each other down, and I toed off my shoes as Trent led me further into the room without pulling away from the kiss.

"How far do you want to take this?" Trent panted.

I gave him an incredulous look. "Just hurry," I said in urgency. "I don't care, just whatever it is we're doing, hurry it."

I could have probably stated my case better, but the only thing left in my mind was getting him above me in bed, naked. I knew where this was leading; I was old enough to do it even if I'd never tried it before.

He stopped and pulled away long enough when we got to the bedroom to take off his shoes, socks, and pants. I was already down to my underwear and stood impatiently beside the bed, biting down on my lower lip as I watched him strip. He stalked over to me, and all I could do was stare at his body, until he was right in front of me, pulling off my bra and panties.

We tumbled onto the bed, hands groping all over, mouths leaving wet kisses everywhere we could reach. We stopped with Trent braced above me, his hips pressed between my open thighs.

How long have I been waiting for this, I thought to myself, as we stopped and our eyes caught. I wanted to say something, to tell him that I'd been waiting for him all this time. But the space between us was so delicate at that moment. I felt like if I spoke he would stop, and I didn't want to stop now that we'd come this far.

I could feel his cock, hot and hard, pressing against my thigh, and I had a moment of fear. Just what was I doing? I'd been saving myself for this man, but just to give it up in an impulsive moment could only come back to bite me in the ass.

But I didn't stop him. He lowered his upper body on his arms, pressing his forehead against mine and holding my eyes as he swiveled his hips. I shivered, feeling the head of his cock sliding between my wet folds without actually entering me.

"Trent," I moaned, squirming under him, trying to take him inside of me.

He smirked down at me, and I squirmed some more as he moved his hips, searching. The head of his cock found my entrance at last, and I held my breath as he pushed relentlessly forward. There was a frown on his face when he was met with some resistance, but he didn't stop, and I gasped when I felt a quick flash of pain. Trent didn't notice the pain twisting my expression; his own eyes had slid shut.

"Shit," he hissed through gritted teeth. He threw his head back, and I watched the cords in his throat strain as he slowly slid into me. "You're so tight, Jessi."

Well, yes, I thought hysterically. It is my first time, after all!

But all I could do was clutch onto his biceps, my nails digging into his flesh, thankful he was at least careful with me. He bottomed out and paused so we could breathe. He opened his eyes again and looked down to meet my gaze.

I'm doing it, I thought. I'm having sex with Trent Thompson!

I couldn't describe my excitement, my happiness in that moment. I'd forgotten all about how I didn't like him, didn't want to see him. My eyes stung with tears.

Then he started to move, and I thought I would shatter.

9

TRENT

I'd been trying to get her out of my head all day. I wasn't the type of guy to ponder. Fuck! I never did that, but with Jessi, the more I tried to get her out of my mind, the more she popped back into it. I felt like some lovesick teenager and I hated it. It was as if she was taunting me on purpose, because the moment I did finally go through a good couple of hours of not thinking about her, it was brought to a dramatic end as I bumped into her.

Instead, I'd let myself get lost in her expression. I hadn't seen her for years, and sudden longing hit me to have her in my arms, no matter how accidental. She wasn't pulling away from me either, and because of that I wasn't immediately pushing her away. In fact, my instincts in that moment were begging for me to pull her closer to me instead.

So sweet, I thought. So intoxicatingly sweet, the one thing about her that hadn't changed over the years.

She had changed though, so much. And now, with her held in my arms, there was no running from it.

Her hair was a light blonde-brown, falling to her waist, parted in the middle and pushed back away from her face. Before, she'd had bangs that hid her face. I approved of the hairstyle change, and hoped she'd done it realizing she'd never needed to hide in the first place; she'd always been beautiful, she'd only grown more so.

Jessi's eyes were a light brown that was made that much lighter by the shades in her hair, varying from darkest brown to a golden blond, and they looked like they were dancing every time she smiled. She rarely smiled at me, so I'd only ever got to see the look when it was aimed at other people.

She was also as small as she'd ever been. At five foot five, I was a head taller than her. But the body pressed against mine was nowhere near the skinny, gangly teenager I remembered.

Fuck, I was in trouble.

Jessi was all warm, soft curves, and the moment that sunk into my mind, I knew I needed to pull away before she noticed my body starting to stir. I'd pretty much been half hard the whole day because of her, but I'd got a handle on it until now. It would be too humiliating, even though she looked a little bit tipsy, to let her know just how much she affected me when my first instinct around her was usually to dismiss her.

But she wouldn't let me withdraw. Instead, she kissed me. Only, it wasn't the same innocent press of lips as before, her tongue sliding into my mouth at my gasp of surprise. Then I was kissing her back.

She was too sweet to resist, and I gave into my decades of longing for something warm and wonderful, just this once. There would be repercussions, but I could deal with them later.

Minutes later, I had her in my room, in my bed and under me as I slid into her.

It felt amazing…

It was hardly my first time having sex. I'd lost my virginity pretty early on because I didn't think it was anything too important to hold onto. Though it might have been my imagination, it was different with Jessi.

She moaned under me, her legs tightening around my waist as her nails dug into my lower back. My eyes fluttered open as my head ducked down, and I caught her eyes.

"What is it?" I whispered, moving my hips just slightly, and watching in fascination as her eyes widened and she let out a few gasps as she squirmed again.

It affected me too, of course, and I couldn't help letting out a low groan as I moved some more.

I want this to last.

The thought was a surprise when it popped into my mind, but I went with it. I moved one of my forearms to brace myself up on the other one, and wrapped an arm around Jessi's waist, lifting her hips slightly. I moved in slow thrusts, circling my hips as I did, searching for all her hot spots.

"Fuck," I muttered.

I hid my face in her shoulder, realizing we hadn't had

much foreplay. It was such a damn waste because it would have been so much more fun if I could have taken my time to make her go crazy with lust before I fucked her. I'd skipped a few steps in my impatience.

There's always next time, I thought, and grinned.

"Trent," Jessi said through her pants, nails digging even harder into my back to the point I thought she wanted to draw blood on purpose.

I hummed to let her know I was listening but didn't stop kissing all over her cheek and down to her neck, pausing here and there for a nip and a light suck. I had a moment where I was tempted to leave some mark on her. The impulse was so strong I almost did it and only managed not to by pulling myself away at the last minute.

We both worked at the hotel, but I knew it would be harder for Jessi to explain the kind of mark I wanted to leave.

"I loved it especially when you were moving," she admitted. "Can we please go back to that?"

I chuckled and nipped on her chin.

"Whatever you want, Jessi," I murmured, then moved.

Her reaction was immediate, gasping moans falling out of her mouth as she squirmed and writhed underneath me. I smirked devilishly down at her as I moved my hips in slow, deep thrusts. Enough to drive her crazy, but not enough to get her to come. I'd skipped the foreplay, so I'd at least make this part last. I wouldn't let her see just how much effort it was taking for me to go slow, though. I was barely hanging on by a thread.

"Trent!" she cried out, with more urgency in her tone.

A shiver went down my back when she called my name like that. I let out a low growl as I started to move just a little bit faster. I moved the arm I was still bracing myself down with, instead of wrapping it around Jessi's shoulders. I carefully lay my weight down on top of her, but she didn't protest. Just moaned and squirmed some more.

I groaned as I moved just a little bit faster. Her warm, wet walls trembled around my cock with every one of my thrusts, and I picked up the pace a little bit at a time. I placed kisses all over her face, down her cheek to her neck, pausing to place a kiss just beneath her ear. The kisses continued down her neck, and I bowed my back a little to continue down her chest until I found one of her breasts.

"Would you like me to touch you here?" I asked.

I didn't need to. She was practically holding her breath as she waited for me, but I would let her wait until I got an answer to my question. I licked teasing circles around the top of her breasts, moving down a bit, only to slide back up.

"Hurry up," she moaned, one of her hands sliding up from my back to tangle in my hair and tug on it. I grinned at her skin as I let her guide me where she wanted me.

"Tell me what you want me to do," I whispered, glancing up at her.

She met my gaze. Her cheeks were flushed, lips swollen from my kisses and panting for breath. She looked so damn delectable that I wanted to ravish her whole.

"Here," she said softly, pushing my head tentatively down on her breasts as she arched her back just a little. "I need you, right here."

At that, my focus returned to where it had been before. I licked a careful circle around one pink nipple as her body shuddered out a sigh. I looked up to meet her eyes again as I flicked the tip of my tongue on her nipple. The shock was obvious on her face, her eyes widening as her mouth fell slack. I did it again, and again, watching her face the whole time. Then I circled my mouth around her nipple and sucked gently.

"Just like that," she groaned, tipping her head back and pushing her breasts into my face. "Feels so good…"

Encouraged by her breathy sighs, I moved my ministrations to her other breast, sucking harder on it, then rolling it gently between my teeth and licking it. I teased at her nipples until they were both flushed and a little swollen. I was tempted to continue, but I didn't want to hurt her.

I kissed my way up the valley between her breasts, up her throat, over her chin, and to her mouth. She melted into my kiss

I let out a groan of my own as I held her close and thrust faster into her. My last thread of control was pretty much broken. She looked too good under me for me to draw this out for long, and I started fucking her in earnest, pulling louder moans and cries from her lips that only made me move faster. I held her close and fucked her hard, burying my face in her shoulder and biting down on her neck.

"Trent!"

I hissed at how she said my name, all desperate and wanting to come. I loved it, and it pushed me that much closer to the edge. I could feel sparks of electricity shooting up and down my spine, and I knew I was drawing close. I listened to Jessi's gasping breaths and cries. She had to come before I did, and with my focus on that, I slammed my hips against hers as I fucked her even harder, just that little bit faster, grinding myself into her clit to give that added pleasurable friction.

Jessi let out a short scream as her body seized up in my arms. Then her walls were convulsing hard around my cock as she shuddered through her orgasm. Letting out a growl, my hips slammed against hers in a few harsh, erratic thrusts, and I went still as I hit my climax. We held each other close, then slumped into the bed as we calmed down. I rolled us over so I wouldn't crush her into the mattress, loosening my hold.

"Wow," I murmured, burying my face in her hair, taking in her scent, then pulling back to grin down at her.

She stared at me, dazed. "What?"

I chuckled. "That was amazing, and I'm glad you agree. Look at you, all speechless."

She blinked up at me.

I tugged the covers over the both of us. We were both covered in a light sheen of sweat, and I knew she'd start to feel the chill as it cooled down. My legs shifted, and I winced when I felt my limp, wet cock against my thigh.

"Give me a minute," I grumbled, moving to get out of the bed.

But Jessi didn't let me get far, her hand clutching at my bicep to keep me still.

"Wait!" she cried out, only to squirm under the covers when she realized she'd been a little loud.

I grinned at her cute antics. "What is it?" I asked, brushing a lock of hair away from her face.

"Where are you going?" she asked.

My chest swelled a little in pride. She didn't want me going anywhere. The thought made me break out into a larger grin, and I couldn't remember the last time I was this happy, or entertained, while in bed with someone. Usually, by this point, either I or the woman would be getting out of bed and getting ready to leave.

But why did Jessi look so shifty?

"I'm not going anywhere," I reassured her. "I was just going to get something to clean us both up."

I hadn't used a condom, I realized. I didn't exactly have any on me because I'd come home with clear goals in mind, and sex had never been in that set of goals. I had to hope she was protected and go about the business of bringing her a towel to clean up.

"It's fine," she said quickly, tugging on the hold she had on my arm.

I frowned but decided I didn't need to go anywhere after all. I watched as she sighed and closed her eyes, snuggling into my pillow. A minute later, her breathing had slowed down and evened out, and I knew she'd fallen asleep, but I couldn't take my eyes off of her. There was something peaceful about the way she slept as if everything that was wrong had all of a sudden disappeared and it brought a smile to my face just watching her.

When did you get this beautiful, Jessi?

I knew the truth was that she always had been. She was just more grown up now. I hadn't expected she'd ever wind up in my bed though. Or just how much I'd loved having her in it.

It would have been wonderful if I could have something like this. I knew it was impossible, but I indulged myself in it just a bit. If I hadn't been so stuck up when she confessed to me when we were young, or if I had returned her kiss then we would have been together. We'd have got married and already started a family together. It was something I didn't see in the cards for my future, but the thought of a family with Jessi sounded divine for some reason.

Why couldn't it happen? I questioned myself for the first time.

I pulled her close, tucking her into my chest. She let out a sigh, her arms going around me as she ducked her head under my chin. I closed my eyes, buried my face in her hair, and inhaled her scent again.

Like that, we fell asleep, and I felt peace for the first time I could remember without having to resort to sleeping pills. I couldn't help but dream of all the things I could have with Jessi.

When I woke up in the morning, she was gone.

10

JESSI

$\mathcal{I}$ woke up feeling a little strange—as if I'd been taken captive by aliens, but I knew there were two reasons for me feeling this way.

I was really warm, almost uncomfortably warm, and I was sweating slightly as I traced a finger on my sheets. The other issue was the fact my head was hurting so much. It was an uncontrollable pain, as if my head was about to explode. I tried to move my head, but I couldn't because it felt as if it was an erupting volcano.

What the fuck was I thinking last night? I thought to myself with a light groan.

I didn't often drink, even when it was wine. The most I'd ever had was when some of the pastries I made needed wine in them. Like my parents, I took the occasional champagne at a party, and wine was saved for special occasions.

And yet, Laura and I had gone through two bottles last night, which I would have to remember to replace before the rest of the staff realized, or I'd be in some serious trouble because they were both expensive bottles. Not only was I hung over, my skin felt icky with dried sweat, and the inside of my mouth tasted disgusting.

I couldn't even remember most of what she and I had talked about and I wondered if I'd told her anything particularly incriminating. We were having fun, and it was the first time for me in a long time, so I'd let myself go.

Regret curled into my stomach now. Not only regret, I realized, as my stomach gurgled and I had a moment where I was worried the wine and cake from last night would come right back up. I frowned and curled in on myself as much as I could, swallowing down the need to vomit. The wave of nausea passed, and I let out a sigh.

But then, there was a third thing. I was in a bed that wasn't my own because it was too large and soft. There was also the fact I wasn't alone in it. In fact, I couldn't curl up much when I tried, because I was being held close to a body larger than mine by strong arms.

My memories from last night weren't all gone, and I knew who I would see when I opened my eyes. I didn't want to, just yet, because I knew the moment I did, I would want to run away.

But my curiosity won out. After a minute of debating with myself, I let my eyes flutter open, and there he was.

Trent. I was lying in bed wrapped in Trent's arms.

It was a dream come true, even though teenage me had thought it would be so much more innocent. Nevertheless, Trent was holding me close enough that I knew he was completely naked. And so was I.

My body started to heat up all on its own as memories from last night bombarded my thoughts.

Oh, shit.

I was tempted to squirm but I didn't want to wake him up.

Why not, though?

I paused at the thought, realizing I did want to wake him up. The thoughts from last night were all wonderful, but I wanted more than just a memory. I wanted to shake him awake. I wanted to feel him between my thighs once more, his cock inside me, filling me up and moving deliciously in ways that drove me crazy with lust. I wanted to kiss him again, taste his silky skin one more time.

Not that I could kiss him with the way my mouth tasted. With my head still aching slightly and my body feeling so icky. There was something uncomfortable between my thighs when I shifted them, and I thought it would be better if I could have a bath and brush my teeth first. Maybe gargle some mouthwash to get rid of the disgusting taste in my mouth.

So, no waking Trent up for some morning fun. I would be too awkward about it anyway, with last night being my first time and all. I remembered him remarking I was tight and hoped he hadn't realized that fact.

But more than that, I knew it was a mistake.

I bumped into him and seduced him last night. We both got lost in the moment, but he would regret it when his eyes opened and he saw who was lying next to him.

Before that happened, I had to be gone.

This was all my fault. I couldn't say I'd been plastered

last night, but I hadn't exactly been sober either. Running into him was one thing, and I didn't know where the courage to kiss him even came from, but I knew he would blame me for coming on to him.

I'd had enough shit from this guy as it was. Thinking of the fallout from last night's activities was enough to make my stomach churn some more.

This shouldn't have happened at all. I rubbed my thighs together, feeling uncomfortable at the soreness between my legs, only to freeze when I remembered what it meant.

We didn't use protection last night.

Shit!

With sudden urgency, I started to move. I did so carefully, doing my best not to wake him. His arms slid out from around me, and I got off the side of the bed, standing up. Almost immediately, I was falling, but I managed to hold onto the bed and brace myself so I wouldn't end up on the floor. My legs were just a little wobbly, but what surprised me was how sore I felt between my legs. How had I not noticed that?

I winced as I straightened up once more, better prepared now. I walked around the room, looking for my dropped clothes, and pulling them all on, grimacing at how disgusting I felt. I needed to get back to my room and take a shower.

Fully dressed, I tiptoed out of the room, taking a last glance at Trent sleeping peacefully before I ran.

Back in my room, I tossed my clothes off and went straight to the shower. I ducked under the spray before it could warm up and I stood under it, letting the water wash over me and sluice away the aches.

I was panicking.

We didn't use any protection last night!

I was a virgin, and I'd had myself tested before. There was no worry on my end, and while I didn't know about Trent because he wasn't a celibate, I had to believe he probably took care of himself. That controlling personality of his wouldn't allow for anything less, would it?

But there was another, bigger worry, and I didn't know what to do with it.

"What happens if I get pregnant?" I said to myself, my voice hushed.

I hadn't been on any contraceptives before because I didn't have a sex life. So last night had come out of nowhere. I knew there were pills I could take, the morning after pills. I just didn't know if I could bring myself to take them? Could I bring myself to do that to a possible pregnancy? The thought of being pregnant was a little daunting in my current position, but I was even more worried about what would happen if I did nothing about the possibility.

What was I going to do?

The question whirled around in my mouth as I washed myself thoroughly, grimacing when I caught some spots of red when I washed between my thighs. I washed up twice and rinsed, then stepped out, wrapping a towel around my body and another one around my hair.

I stopped in front of my bathroom mirror and stared at my reflection. It had been a while since I'd last looked at myself, and I realized I had changed. My face looked the same, but after last night, I was no longer a virgin, and it was something I would never get back.

Not that I regretted it. I'd been saving it for the right man, and for me, that had always been Trent.

"But I need to take care of the consequences," I told myself firmly.

There was only one decision I could make. If Trent found out I was pregnant, would he even let me explain? What happened if he didn't care and walked away? He would hate me, and he would never forgive me if I ended up pregnant from our one-night stand. Trent would never ever forgive me.

"I need the pill." The words came out in a harsh whisper, and the look of horror that crossed my face was exactly how I felt in my chest.

After drying up, I looked for new clothes to pull on. I picked up a t-shirt and jeans, then pulled a hoodie on top, pulling the hood down to cover my face. I pulled on my sneakers then picked up my purse and left.

There was a pharmacy a short distance from the hotel. It was close enough to walk. I went slowly anyway, but ten minutes later, I was exchanging cash for the pills I would need.

"Here you go," the girl behind the counter said, grinning up at me. "Next time you need a plan so you don't need the emergency pills. A lot of women don't like taking them. You need to see a doctor to set up a contraception plan."

I gave her a pained smile. "Thanks for the advice," I murmured as I walked away.

I wasn't hiding the fact I was ashamed of what I was

doing, and it was nice of her to take the time to explain it to me. I could have just stopped and thought about using condoms last night and I wouldn't be in the position I was in, I reminded myself. I'd been a virgin last night, but I hadn't been an idiot, so the fault was completely my own.

On the walk back to the hotel, I moved even slower, contemplating this step I was about to take. I shouldn't have treated sex so lightly in the first place, no matter how caught up in the moment I was, and this was kind of like my punishment. I kept going back and forth about what to do. By the time I made it to my room, I knew what I was going to do, and my eyes were already stinging with tears.

I went to my kitchen and got a glass of water, then sat with it on my small counter. I took five whole minutes staring at the glass of water and the pills before I removed one from the sheet with trembling hands.

"I'm doing this," I whispered to the empty room. My eyes dropped down to my tummy, and I placed one trembling hand over it, blinking back another wash of tears. "I'm so sorry."

With that apology, I picked up the pill, threw it into my mouth, and swallowed it down with the water.

An hour later, it was time for my shift. I'd taken another quick shower and dressed in a different set of clothes. I headed down to the staffroom where the lockers were located and pulled on my white coat. I tied back my hair and tucked it under my chef's hat.

What am I going to do? I thought again.

There was no way I could ever face Trent again, not after last night. Not after I'd thrown myself at him like that.

He was already an asshole to me at the best of times; his smirking was going to be astronomical after this!

I couldn't deal with it. It had been hard enough having him laugh at me for a chaste kiss. Him making fun of me after we'd slept together… any bit of self-esteem I managed to gather while he was gone would go down the drain.

Should I quit? I wondered to myself. It might be for the best. I'd have to move someplace else. Maybe back in with my parents? There'd be no reason for us to meet as long as I kept to the servant halls and entries and exits.

I didn't want to be a bother to my parents, though. Besides, they'd ask why I was suddenly so eager to move back home when I'd been just as eager to leave after high school.

Or, I thought, brainstorming, I could always try moving to another location. The hotel has several branches, and I was offered a job at any of the others…

It would mean going far away from my parents. I'd decided to stay in Charlotte because I didn't want to be away from them. But there was nothing else I could do, was there? I'd do anything if it meant getting away from Trent and seeing that smirk of his ever again.

My mind drifted to thoughts of last night. I remembered the soft touches he'd placed on my shoulder, the sweet way he'd kissed me. But I knew I couldn't think of it as making love. To Trent, we'd fucked, and that was it. Everything I'd imagined in my mind didn't mean anything to him. And it shouldn't mean anything to me either.

Trent was a dick, I'd known it for a while. What had been so beautiful to me would just be another weapon in his arsenal, and I was not going to stick around for him to use it against me.

I had a feeling if he ever did use it, it would be enough to destroy me. I could leave after he'd done it, or I could do it before, and I knew which I was going to pick for the sake of my self-preservation.

I'm sorry Mom and Dad, I thought, sending out another round of apologies. I know I'd been the one to make the promise, but it looks like I'm going to go far away.

I was determined, and as I went to work, I wasn't distracted.

11

TRENT

The bed felt empty and cold as I struggled to open my eyes. My legs and arms slowly moved across the mattress, only to discover I was alone.

Where did she go?

I listened out with a stirring of hope. Maybe she was in the bathroom or something? But after a minute of listening and catching nothing, I gave it up and sighed, sitting up in bed.

"Jessi?" I tried calling out, not expecting an answer.

Fuck.

Why wouldn't she be there when I woke up? After last night I'd hoped things had changed between us. Maybe not?

"Maybe I'm thinking too much," I grumbled to myself. "I need to talk to Jessi first."

I nodded to myself as I made the decision. It would be the smart thing to do, after all.

Decision made, I crawled out of bed, slowly taking one

step at a time. I threw the covers to the side and frowned, then looked down at myself.

"Shit! Was I too rough last night?"

Jessi hadn't said anything, but suddenly I felt very concerned.

I headed to the bathroom to get showered. I got out with a towel around my waist, another around my shoulder that I used to dry my hair. I went to my closet and looked at my clothes. There wasn't much, and I thought about either having more brought from my home or buying more. Someone would be coming to clean my room and they would take the clothes I'd thrown all over the floor, so I didn't try to pick them up. Then I looked over at the bed and hesitated.

No, it's fine, I thought. No one would think of Jessi, so it shouldn't be a problem.

I hoped that was true as I picked out my suit for the day, then started to get dressed. Underwear first, then the slacks and shirt. After picking out a pair of cufflinks, I pulled on the suit coat and fixed up the tie before buttoning up the coat. I took a look at myself in the mirror, then styled my hair so the bangs were pushed away from my forehead. It took a bit of gel, but my hair was usually good at behaving.

Properly dressed, I stepped out of my room. The first thing I wanted to do was to run around and look for Jessi, but I knew I couldn't do that. There was still a lot of work to do, and besides, people would talk if I went to find her straight away. It would be best for the both of us if I had some strength of will.

"Later," I promised myself, heading up to the office. "I'll look for her later."

I missed her, though.

The thought was enough to startle me, though I didn't let it show visibly as I found an elevator. I wasn't the only one waiting for one, but the others were likely guests hoping to go down for breakfast. When both elevators opened, I hesitated, but when I got inside the one going up, the guests went for the other one.

Why Jessi had left my bed this morning was still on my mind. And the fact I missed her, but I had to get on with my day.

Maybe I'll go see her in the evening? I thought. I wasn't sure where her room was. But she worked in the building so maybe I could try the staff room again? It wouldn't take much sleuthing to find out where her room was.

Put it out of your mind for now, I thought to myself as I came up to the office. You've got important work to do.

The secretary had a desk outside the office, and as I came up, she rose to her feet with hands clasped in front of her as she gave me a polite smile.

"Good morning, sir."

"Good morning," I muttered back, distracted. Then I focused on her with a frown. "Have breakfast sent up to me, please. And call the management, see if they've found that paperwork I asked them to look at before."

I was still looking at some of the accounting records for the hotel, among other things. It was the most important thing I wanted to look into. There was nothing wrong with what I'd seen so far, but I was meticulous—as Dad had taught all his children to be—so I wasn't leaving anything out. Even though it was a bit overkill and I was starting to feel the effects of my late nights and early morning starts.

"Right away, sir," the secretary said readily. "Anything specific you want for breakfast?"

That made me pause. Usually, I just had coffee, and that was it. But…

"Have some coffee sent up and a pastry. Whatever you think I'd like best, but nothing too sweet."

"Yes, sir," she said with a bobbing nod.

I walked into the office, frowning to myself. I didn't pick a pastry because Jessi was the primary pastry chef in the hotel. I was just… tasting what the hotel had to offer. I also pushed aside the fact I wanted to see her again. That was just… because of last night, so she could explain to me exactly what went down and how she ended up in my arms.

Should I ask how she ended up in my bed, too? I pushed the thought aside.

I took off my coat and laid it on the back of my chair as usual. Then I sat down and pulled the folders I'd left on the desk last night closer to me. I did a quick perusal of them. About ten minutes later there was a knock on my door, and I looked up, closing the folder I'd just finished with.

"Come in, please," I called.

The secretary opened the door, and someone with a uniform from the hotel kitchens pushed a tray inside. I caught myself thinking it could have been Jessi and pushed the thought out of my mind. It was probably not her job to move food around, just to make it.

The staff worker stopped the tray beside my desk and transferred it from the trolley he was pushing. There was a mug and a carafe of coffee, and under the tray were a few pastries. It wasn't something I often ate so I didn't recognize what was on the plate. The staff worker left it all in front of me, gave a short bow, then made his way out.

I didn't get immediate word from my secretary about the lower management and the paperwork I needed. I wondered if they were even awake and if I'd need to change business hours, so they could be in their offices when they were needed.

That would only be convenient for me, I decided. Besides, the old man would probably get mad if I messed things up for him before he got back.

I poured the coffee and took a sip, then eyed the plate of pastries. After some thought, I picked a small, round one that had a slight hollow at the top. I bit into it, paused, then chewed. I nodded slowly to myself as I took another bite of it. The bread had just the right level of crunch without being too flaky and breaking off in my fingers, it was slightly sweet, and it had melted cheese in the middle.

I wanted the name of it. It tasted so good it seemed a waste that I hadn't been taking it every day with my coffee. When had I decided black coffee alone would be a good breakfast? I'd been missing out. I finished the first pastry then took another, and another. By the time the plate and my mug were empty, I was tempted to lick my fingers. I looked up, realized I was alone and did it anyway.

Afterward, I grumbled to myself for doing something

so un-classy, whether or not someone was watching me do it, and wiped my fingers on a napkin.

The secretary chose that moment to come in, and I was relieved she hadn't come in just a few seconds earlier. She'd knocked first, but then I wouldn't need to have a guilty expression on my face that would clue her in.

"Yes?" I said as she stepped up to the desk.

"I spoke to the manager and he said he'd be passing by the accounting and financial departments and have someone bring up the documents for you. You should have them in an hour. Was there anything else you needed?"

I frowned because what I needed was those documents a lot earlier than an hour. It would seem there was nothing I could do about it and there was no use in complaining.

"No," I said. "Just let me know when they come in, thank you."

I gave her a dismissive nod, but she blinked at me a couple of times in surprise. I frowned, wondering if it was because I hadn't made a complaint about the tardiness. Did I always do that? Well, whatever. I gave her a pointed look, and her expression turned sheepish before she walked out of the room.

Alone again, I poured myself more coffee and took my time with it. I pulled the files I was looking through before breakfast came. Since it was just a quick perusal, I did it at my leisure, feeling relaxed for the first time in a long while. I had an hour to do that before getting down to serious work.

At the moment, I found my thoughts drifting back to Jessi, and I frowned slightly. It was strange, how I felt about her after last night. She wasn't the first woman I'd had a one-night stand with, so why was I still thinking about her? She'd been in my thoughts on and off for over a decade, but last night should have got her out of my system.

There was a part of me that felt terrified. I wasn't sure if last night was a one-night stand to Jessi, and I hoped not because I did want to see her again. I wasn't sure I wanted to sleep with her again—okay, that was a lie, I just didn't know if I was going to—but I would be looking for her at my earliest convenience.

Oddly, no matter how terrified I should probably feel that I wanted to see her again, I was calm. It was only sex, after all. We had been good in bed together, Jessi and me. That had been unexpected, and I was wondering what it would be like if we did it again with a bit more knowledge about each other now.

Only sex, I thought to myself. I would want more of that.

Another knock on my door brought me out of my revelry, and I looked up as the secretary walked in with two people behind her. One of them had come for the tray, while the other had come with an armful of folders that were set on the edge of the desk.

Had an hour passed already? I'd barely noticed. I finished my coffee so my mug could be taken down with everything else.

"These are all the relevant files you'll need, sir," the secretary said. "Will there be anything else?"

I shook my head as I pulled the pile closer. "No, all this is fine. I'll let you know if I need anything more."

With that, she walked out and left me alone again. I started up the computer to access the company database so I could look through the documents and match them to the information we had in the database. Tomorrow, if I still had no word from Dad, I'd start looking into his planned meetings.

I spent the day working, going through my business and Dad's. Jessi drifted out of my mind, and I lost track of time. It was hours later when I pushed back into the seat, clenching and unclenching my fists.

My mind, of course, drifted right back to Jessi.

I wanted to see her. More than that, I wanted to talk to her. I wasn't sure if she'd feel the same, but hopefully, I could convince her not to keep avoiding me. Things had changed for us now. My behavior toward her had been nothing more than a cover before, and there was no reason to keep it up anymore.

Maybe… Could I take her out to dinner?

With the thought in mind, the first thing I wanted to do was call my PA. I had to remind myself she wasn't with me at the hotel, even though she was the one who usually set things up for me. So instead, I called for the secretary. She was in my room seconds later.

"I want you to look into someone for me," I said before she could start. "Her name is Jessi, she works as the pastry chef in the kitchen. I know she lives in the hotel, but I'm not sure where. Just get me as much about her as you can find, all right?"

She nodded, hiding a look of confusion. "Of course, sir. And I also wanted to let you know, that I've received a few calls. I know you wanted any meetings to wait, but a major partner of the hotel is coming down to see you. He said it was something important. There was also more than one call like that. Should I send them all away?"

I pursed my lips, thinking. Should I? There was a reason I was ignoring my dad's meetings. I didn't know his plans, and I didn't want to accidentally put a wrench in them. But if they were all already on their way then I might as well. Besides, I'd tried to talk to Dad and he wouldn't see me. So if anything went wrong it wasn't my fault I was going in with no information. He wasn't there to give it to me.

"It's fine," I said. "Just get me the information."

"Yes, sir."

That was how I found the rest of my day spent in meetings. I knew I should be paying complete attention, but I had no idea what was going on in each of them. I barely heard a word anyway.

Instead, I thought about Jessi and last night. I thought about how she'd sighed as I touched her, all high and breathy, just at the edge of a whine. The way she would hiss, fingertips digging into my back, as I fucked her into the mattress. The way she had looked at me, cheeks flushed, and swollen lips opened wide—her light brown eyes with a wet sheen in them—as she came, writhing under me. I couldn't help stealing a glance at that look before I'd buried my face in her shoulder for my orgasm.

Fuck.

I want her again, I admitted to myself. There was no point trying to deny it, was there? During lunch, I called for another of her pastries as a dessert with my meal, and it kept her in my mind through the rest of the day. I was half hard through most of my meetings, but thankfully, it all happened in the office, and I was hidden by the desk.

I left the office at my usual time, but I'd got quite a bit done, not including the meetings. The secretary had retrieved the information I wanted, and I couldn't help rushing to Jessi's quarters. It was a bit late, but considering how late she was out yesterday, it probably wouldn't be a problem. I would have wanted to come sooner, but I couldn't allow myself to shirk my duties for any reason, it just wasn't professional. I'd already called down, and Jessi wasn't in the kitchens or the staff room.

After a moment to catch my breath, I knocked on the door. I waited a minute, but no answer. I knocked again, pressing my ear closer to the door.

"Jessi?" I called, feeling a bit awkward. "It's me, Trent. I was wondering if we could talk, maybe?"

I wasn't getting an answer and I didn't know why. Five minutes of waiting made me decide she was either not home, or she just didn't want to talk to me.

She had been in love with me for years. Or at least, she had been years ago. Maybe I wanted more of her, but... maybe she'd had her fill of me?

That couldn't be it, could it?

12

JESSI

$\mathcal{I}$ worked through the day, half in a daze. By the time my shift had finished, I'd decided there was no way I was going back to my apartment. Trent would know where it was, and the last thing I needed at that moment was to risk running into him again.

So once my shift was over, I moved to the staff room and called for Laura, who must have also finished her shift. Sure enough, minutes after my call, she walked into the room. I jumped a little, still worked up from that day Trent had walked in here with absolutely no warning. I did not need a repeat of that.

I didn't need to see Trent, period. There was no way I could face him.

"Hey there, Jessi," Laura said, practically skipping into the room.

I frowned at her. "Hey, Laura. You're in a good mood today."

She sighed then plopped down on the couch beside me.

Her legs stretched out as she laid her arms on the back of the couch, head tilted back with a smile on her lips as she closed her eyes.

"Well, I woke up this morning feeling wonderful, and it's just been the same through the day. I caught sight of Mason around earlier, but there were no parties today! That's enough for me to want to have my own party."

I watched her with a skeptical eyebrow arched, one she didn't see because she was busy giggling to herself. I pursed my lips, feeling a little annoyed that she was this happy when it felt like my world was crumbling around me. That wasn't fair, so I kept my bad mood to myself.

She seemed to sense it anyway, a small frown appearing on her face as she peered at me out the corner of her eyes.

"Why are you so quiet?" she wondered.

I rolled my eyes and then laughed. "Maybe because not all of us had sunshine and rainbows through the whole day? We were drinking together last night; how did you not wake up with a hangover like me?"

She blinked. "Well, what happened was this. I had a bit of water before I left, and the taxi let me off a block away from my place."

Immediately, I sat up, eyes wide with worry. "Did something happen?"

Laura giggled again, waving a hand at me. "Don't worry so much, silly. I can look after myself, don't you know. But I did stop by somewhere to have a bite to eat, just some pasta with some really good sauce. Then I had more water, and I walked the rest of the way back to my apartment in the chilly night air. I was pretty much sobered up by the time I got home."

I sighed, slumping back into my side of the couch. "Then I guess I should have gone with you last night. It would have been the best-case scenario for me."

So much better than what did happen. Well, maybe not better, but it would have been the best thing to happen. Not that I could regret what happened between Trent and me completely. I just needed to avoid him now and act like nothing had happened in the first place.

"Did something happen?" Laura asked, sitting up suddenly now and frowning at me. "I wanted to talk to you this morning, see how you were, but I was running a bit late for my shift, and I didn't have the time to come see you all day. Was your hangover this morning really bad?"

I grimaced. "You have no idea, Laura. It was terrible." Even if it wasn't necessarily the hangover, but waking up somewhere unexpected, and having thoughts that were more like dreams that would never come true, no matter how much I wished. "I'm not drinking wine for some time after last night."

"Did you replace the wine bottles already?"

I nodded. I'd found some time in the middle of the day to make an order for the exact same bottles to be brought in. They'd cost just as much as I'd feared, an extra cost added on top of the delivery. At least it was one less thing for me to worry about, and anyway, I saved most of my salary since my parents didn't need it. Most of my costs were only food and a few clothes and shoes a month, so there was a nice cushion in my bank account.

"Yeah, I don't think anybody noticed they were missing anyway. We don't break out the wine for that many occasions, do we?"

Laura tilted her head slightly to the side. "Then why is there so much of it just lying around?"

I shrugged. "Wine doesn't have an expiration date, remember? No one's gonna care how long it's lying around. Most of the bottles in storage I've never even tasted in all the time I've been working here."

"Me either," she admitted. She'd already been at the hotel when I was transferred, so she'd been there longer than me. "Oh! You called me down for something. Did you want to do something else again tonight?"

I slowly nodded. "Actually, yeah. Nothing to do with alcohol," I said quickly. "Dealing with a hangover is annoying, it's also why I rarely drink at all. But I was thinking, I could maybe come over to your place tonight for a sleepover? I'll cook," I added.

Her eyes lit up at that last bit. "If you'll cook for me, I don't mind taking you home with me. You'd be the most useful thing I ever dragged back to my house."

"Uh-huh," I muttered, giving her a wide-eyed look, full of teasing censure. "Just how many guys do you drag to your home then, huh?"

She giggled. "I don't drag them, they come willingly. And I've been too busy with work to bring anyone home anyway, so don't be so freaked out, I was just kidding. Do you want to stop by your apartment and get something to wear for tomorrow?"

I shrugged. "There's not much I need. I can just get back

early and go change before my shift, so it's not like it matters."

"What if someone sees you? And they think you're doing the whole walk of shame thing, coming home after a one-night stand."

I winced at her words because that was exactly what had happened to me this morning. Only it wasn't such a trip from Trent's room to mine, and I was lucky that it was so early in the morning because I didn't run into anybody. I wasn't going to be repeating it anyway. I just wasn't that kind of girl.

"Can we not talk about that?" I grumbled, getting up from the seat and grabbing her arm to drag her up to me. "Let's head out now. We don't want to be too late."

"It's still early, though!"

I arched an eyebrow at her. "It's already dark out, it's just earlier than when you'd left last night. But I thought getting a walk in might be good. We can walk a bit before taking a taxi."

"Or, we could just walk all the way to my place?"

I winced at that idea. She lived several blocks away and the hotel was big enough to take up two or so blocks. There was no way I would survive a walk that long. Walking from the hotel to the mansion was so much shorter, and it was still quite a walk.

"Let's just find a taxi on the street. If we don't see one, we'll call for one."

Laura laughed at me, and she went to quickly change out of her uniform. Once she was in her street clothes, we headed out through the staff exit, then headed for the street. Laura must have noticed I wasn't acting quite like myself, but she was nice enough not to say anything about it.

We weren't walking for five minutes when a taxi stopped at the curb beside us, the driver honking the horn to catch our attention. Laura teased about walking some more, but I grabbed her hand and dragged her inside with me. She gave the address, and when he dropped us off, I handed him the cash.

"Have you ever been to my place, anyway?" she asked as we made our way up the stairs. Her apartment building was old and didn't have a working elevator.

"Um… I think there was this one time last year? After a staff party, when you were drunk and I brought you back. I ended up staying, but I left before you woke up the next morning."

"Oh," she said, glancing at me over her shoulder and nodding. "I forgot about that. I wondered how I got back in the morning. Thanks for that."

"No problem," I muttered.

We made it to her place, and she unlocked the door to let us in. Her place was even smaller than mine, an open living room and kitchen in the front room, a further door that led to the bathroom and a bedroom.

"You could have gone to your parents, you know," she said, taking off her coat and tossing it and her purse to the single seat.

I sighed. "I don't want to bother my parents. I just need to be away for tonight. From the hotel. If you don't mind?"

She shot me a curious look. "Did something happen that I should know about?"

I hesitated, then shook my head. She probably noticed there was something, but she was nice enough just to nod and head for the kitchen area, waving at me to follow. She wouldn't make me talk about something if I didn't broach the subject myself.

Once again, I was hit by how good a friend Laura was to have around. If I left the hotel, I would miss her.

We spent some time cooking. There weren't many ingredients to work with, but I'd learned to do more than just bake in the kitchen, and I managed to make something nice for us to eat. The room was too small for a dining table, so we sat on the couch and used the coffee table, and Laura turned on the TV.

"Do you think you can wake me up early so we can go together?" she asked.

I nodded. "Sure, no problem."

She hummed, then faced the TV again. I could barely pay attention to what was on, some melodrama that Laura had mentioned before but one I didn't care about. After eating then cleaning up, and the show ending, Laura went to her room to sleep. She left a pillow and some blankets for me, and we both went to sleep. Or I tried to.

I couldn't fall asleep immediately and spent a long time just lying with my eyes open in the dark.

Trent... I didn't want to face him today or any other day. I'd spent the whole day with that fear, and it had grown. I'd started working just fine, but my form had gradually gotten worse until I was so tense, the slightest thing would make me jump. It was a wonder I hadn't accidentally sabotaged my work.

My fear wasn't of Trent, per se. What I was particularly afraid of was being humiliated again by the same guy who'd killed my self-esteem as a teenager. I didn't want history to repeat itself and going by past actions I knew Trent was going to be a complete ass about the whole thing. I couldn't trust my thoughts from last night. We'd both been lost in the moment.

What bothered me was that pill. I was still ashamed and guilty of taking it, and I didn't know why I felt like that. The woman at the pharmacy had said it herself: a lot of women took the morning after pill. But even if Trent couldn't be nice to me, I couldn't face him knowing there was a possibility he could have had a child, and I could have carried it, but my decision pretty much killed that. Literally.

Mom would be so ashamed of me, wouldn't she?

The thought was accompanied by fear. The only solution was to never tell her about it because I didn't want her to be disappointed in me.

But all of it… it became so real for me after I decided to take that pill. I knew Trent could have any woman he wanted. Unlike him, I didn't treat sex as a game. I'd waited for a long time because it meant something to me, and I wanted to give myself to someone special. It wasn't for the sake of any religious beliefs, but because the only man I'd ever wanted was Trent, despite how he'd always treated me.

Now, I'd done it. But because of it, I could never get

near him again, and it made my chest ache.

I didn't think I could fall asleep, but at some point, I must have drifted off. Even as I slept, it was fitful. Trent showed up in my dreams and I'd keep waking up from them drenched in sweat, my body squirming on the couch, either from lust or fear.

By the time it hit the morning hours, I'd barely rested. I turned on Laura's TV, deciding against trying for more sleep. There was some black and white movie playing, and I left it on. Not that I paid attention to it at all.

"I'll have to leave," I muttered to myself. "Definitely."

A couple of hours later, I woke Laura and we got ready to head back to the hotel. She was delaying, so I went ahead. I hurried to the hotel, then to my room to get dressed. I pulled on the most official clothes I had—a blouse and a skirt with a coat pulled over it.

I went to the manager's office for probably the second time since I got hired. He looked up at me, surprised, and I thought he'd only just walked in. It was a bit early, but it didn't matter.

"What can I do for you, today?" he asked, probably recognizing me from the kitchens since he patrolled around the place sometimes. "Is there a problem I can help you with? Is it something to do with the kitchen? It's usually the head chef that comes to me with complaints…"

"It's nothing like that," I said quickly, reassuring him.

"Oh," he sighed, looking relieved. "Good, because with the new guy in upper management, I'd have to take any complaints up to him. What did you want to see me about?"

I clasped my fingers in front of me, twisting them together in a moment of indecision. I thought about how I could barely sleep last night and firmed my resolve.

"I wanted to ask for a transfer to another location," I said. "How soon would that be possible?"

I knew I'd surprised him, but I was more determined in my decision. Just thinking of running into Trent made my heart want to leap out of my chest and run away.

This was the only hope I had if I wanted to get out of this thing between us with some pride left.

13

TRENT

"Damn, this is way too much," I groaned to myself, leaning back in my chair, closing my eyes and rubbing my temples.

"Dude, you're not the only one working here, so stop complaining," Mason called out.

"Yeah," Kevin added. "I only just got here, but you slave drivers are already putting me to work."

"You should have been here to help out sooner," Mason griped.

"I was pretty far out. It took a while to clear things up so I could get here," Kevin retorted.

I let out a loud sigh that had the wonderful side effect of shutting both of them up.

"Could you both keep your mouths shut and keep working? I've been here working longer than the both of you. I was here alone yesterday going through meetings, so if anyone has the right to complain, it's me!"

There were some quiet grumblings of complaint anyway, but it just made me smirk to myself.

I was caught up in work. The first few days there had barely been much to do compared to what we needed to complete today. Even with both my brothers there to help me, there was way too much on my plate, enough to start giving me a headache. It didn't help that I'd been getting calls from my PA back in Nashville. Something had come up that needed my attention, and I didn't have the time to deal with it on top of everything else.

My brothers were at least making themselves useful, but I still felt swamped.

I looked up at them. Mason looked the most like me, though he was the least like me. He had the same grey eyes that I did, his hair a darker blond than mine, and he was only an inch shorter. Kevin didn't look as much like me, with the green eyes he'd gotten from his mother, and light brown hair, though he still had the same features as the rest of us. He was six foot three, a couple of inches shorter than me.

We all had the same physique as our Dad, so it wasn't like I could intimidate them just because I was an inch or so taller. I saw and spoke to Mason a lot more than Kevin. Mason was the partier, and probably the one person in the family who had the most interest in me. Besides Dad, he was the family member I heard from most. He was the last person I'd seen before my decision to come back to Charlotte.

Kevin, though… he and I didn't get along as well. I didn't know how he got along with the rest of the family, but while he was pretty outgoing, he struck me as another isolated soul.

My little half-brother Kevin was what most people would call a free spirit. While I wouldn't quite put it like that, I knew he liked traveling more than staying in one place. Even Mason the partier wasn't quite as bad. And he didn't necessarily go to all the luxurious locations. He'd sent me pictures of the places he visited, and there were about as many pictures of random mountains, forests, and obscure villages as there were cities, hotels, and beaches.

I had always suspected, that of all of us, he would be happy whether he was rich or poor. Kevin was good at finding the bright side of life. Most of his life was spent across the ocean, and he was different from both me and Mason.

"Can I leave you guys with more to do, or will you try to stage a revolt?" I asked.

Their heads jumped up and they sent twin glares at me. They looked a lot more like each other than they looked like me. Besides the slight differences in age, they could have been twins. And they had way more in common. They were both carefree spirits. The difference came in where Mason loved to party, and Kevin just loved to move around.

"You are not leaving us here to go slack off," Mason said, pointing a finger at me. "I don't care how much more you've had to deal with."

"Yeah," Kevin added. "If we're finishing all of this by tonight, we all need to put the effort in."

I rolled my eyes. "Why are you acting as if I'll just drop everything I had on you both? I'm still here and working!"

I sighed and let the matter drop. There was no reason to reduce some of my load by giving it to them. Dad had taught all of us about running a business, but of the three of us, I was the only one who'd been doing it for the past few years. I was used to it so of course, I could work slightly faster.

The only good thing was that there weren't as many documents for today. It was so much easier looking things up online, though it was a bit of a strain on my eyes. I grumbled to myself once more, remembering I'd left my reading glasses in my office back in Asheville. I'd have to call my PA back and have them sent over.

Or, I could just get a new set. If I could find the time to get out of the office.

I lifted my arms, stretching out. Then I got back down to work.

I wondered what Jessi was doing.

The thought slipped through my tight control, and I flattened my lips to keep it to myself, not to alert my brothers that something was wrong. My ensuing problem was that I'd thought her name, and more thoughts of her followed.

I'd been doing so well not to think about her...

I glanced at my brothers, wanting to keep my thoughts private. I kept it all in, pretending I was still paying attention to what I was supposed to be doing, even though I was barely half-interested at this point.

"I'm hungry," Mason declared.

"Me, too," Kevin admitted like I'd expected him to. "Can we take a quick break to eat?"

They both looked at me with pleading expressions.

"You can do what you want. You can get out of the office for a little bit, stretch your legs. Just don't go too far. Let the secretary know to have something sent up to me."

They didn't hesitate to jump out of their seats. I'd had two extra desks brought in for them so I could keep an eye on them and make sure they were working, not just goofing off. I missed the privacy of having the office to myself.

"Are you seriously just going to stay in here for the whole day?" Mason asked, looking a little horrified.

Kevin shrugged. "Probably. You know what Dad is like."

No different from me, I knew. I'd inherited his work ethic. Only, unlike him, I had no one to go home to, so it didn't matter much that I spent so much time at the office. The women I usually met didn't hang around for long.

"Get out of here," I said, waving at them so they would leave. "You better both be back here in an hour, though, or I'll be tracking you down."

They shot me near matching cheeky looks as they left, and I sighed, looking back at my computer.

I groaned to myself after long minutes of not reading what was in front of me. I even gave myself a hard tap on the forehead for good measure. I'd spared Jessi barely a thought here and there before, so how was it that now she was all I could think about?

With my brothers not there to see me lose my mind, I let out a few of my frustrations.

I couldn't get her out of my thoughts, even with all the work I was supposed to be doing. I knew it was bad when work wouldn't distract me like usual.

Jessi… Her beautiful hair, those eyes. The luscious curves of her body that made me want to bury myself in her for hours upon hours…

Focus, Trent! You're the oldest here, you're supposed to be setting a good example.

Still.

It had been a day and I hadn't heard from her at all. It wasn't like she didn't know how to contact me, either. I'd stopped by her room this morning, then gone through the staff room, and I hadn't seen her anywhere.

So where exactly was she? Maybe she'd had what she wanted from me and she was moving on now. I hoped that wasn't the case. I hoped she was just busy, too busy to meet for a chat. She wasn't deliberately ignoring me.

I leaned back in my chair, placed my arms on the armrests, and closed my eyes.

The night we'd had was incredible. She wasn't the usual kind of woman I went for, but I couldn't help wanting more. In some ways, she had been inexperienced, and usually, that was a turn off for me. With Jessi, it had been hot. Maybe it had been a while for her, which would explain the spots of blood if I'd been a bit rough. I just knew there was no way she could have been a virgin, not in this day and age…

Could she?

I frowned as the possibility occurred to me for the first time. I didn't think she could have been, but I'd been thinking a lot about that night we'd been together, and a few more details were coming in clearer.

"It couldn't be possible," I muttered to myself.

I was already grabbing my phone to try and hunt down Emily. I didn't have Jessi's contact number. It had been in the information the secretary had gotten for me, but it would probably be creepy if I just called her up when she hadn't even given me her number. Not to mention just a tad desperate, and that was one thing I was not.

I called the mansion.

"Hello?" someone answered. Probably one of the maids in the house.

"This is Trent; I'm looking for Emily? Is she around?"

"Oh! Mr. Thompson. Um, about Emily, I know she went to see your father earlier, but I believe that was a while ago, for brunch. I couldn't think of where she is now…"

I pursed my lips; a bit irked that Emily got in to see Dad and he was turning me and my brothers down. Was the old man pissed because we were the ones that left home, and she'd been the one to stay?

"Can you look for her and let me know where she is?" I asked.

"Of course, sir. Please hold for a bit."

I was left on hold for a full five minutes before she came back to tell me she'd had no luck.

"Damn," I muttered to myself as I cut the call. "She's going to be harder to find than expected."

If I couldn't find her at home, then finding her wouldn't be easy. When she'd called at my office, I hadn't checked her number. I didn't know if she had my cell number but I didn't have hers. Mason or Kevin might, but then I'd have to ask them about it, and they might ask why I wanted to see her.

They were back before I could manage, and I was pretty sure they hadn't taken the full hour.

"We're back," Mason called out, strutting in first. "Did you miss us?"

Kevin followed after, a kitchen staff member with him.

"We came back with the food," he called out, moving to sit at his desk as the food was brought over to me.

I put my plans on hold, only making quick inquiries here and there to be told when Emily was sighted.

***

I DIDN'T GET anything by the time I went back to my room —after stopping by Jessi's place again, only to get no response.

Then there was a knock on my door. I opened it, surprised to see Emily on the other side.

"I heard you've been looking for me," she said as she side-stepped me and walked into the room.

I gaped at her, and after a second remembered to snap my mouth shut and close the door. I followed her to where she'd moved to drape herself on my couch. I took the single seat that sat diagonally to it and looked at her in disapproval.

"What are you doing here?" I asked, not exactly being polite about it.

She arched an eyebrow at me. "Were you or were you not looking for me all day?"

"I wanted them to let me know when they found you so that we could talk over the phone."

"Or you could have come to the mansion to look for me?" she said, arching an eyebrow. "You do have a room there, don't you?"

I sniffed. "I'm set up in both the mansion and the hotel, but I have more work to do here."

She shrugged. "Fair enough. Now, why did you want to see me?"

I watched her carefully, wondering how to broach the subject. Then decided the direct approach would be best.

"I want to talk about Jessi," I said.

That had her going on the alert. Her gaze was suddenly intense, and she sat up slowly, almost primly, arching an eyebrow at me.

"What about Jessi?"

I took in a deep breath as I settled back, wondering what to say so I wouldn't give too much away.

"For one," I started, "is she seeing anyone? It's been a while since she and I… saw each other. And I was surprised when Dad told me she was working here."

She nodded slowly. "That's right. You've probably known her longer than me, right? You're about the same age."

"We knew each other as kids," I said vaguely. I wasn't very nice to Jessi by the time Emily grew old enough to start to understand things. "You don't have to tell me anything if you don't want to."

She considered me through narrowed eyes for a minute.

"Well, for one, I doubt she's seeing anyone. She's never had a boyfriend that I know of, though there is someone she likes." She folded her arms across her chest and sent me an accusing look. "Jessi is sweet and one of my best friends. I hope you haven't taken advantage of her, big brother, just because the two of you knew each other before. If you're thinking about it, I would ask that you please leave her alone."

Her words were polite, but her tone was hard. It was the first time she'd spoken to me while meeting my gaze, and she didn't look like she was backing down, though neither of us looked away. She held her ground, and I was coming to another realization.

Just what did I think I knew about Emily?

It was all wrong. I didn't know her very well because I'd thought getting information from her would have been the easiest avenue, yet she was looking at me like she would rip me a new one if I did anything to her friend she didn't like.

Well, shit.

I couldn't help feeling impressed at how loyal she was.

"If that was all, brother," she said, getting up. "I'll be going back now."

With a flip of her hair, she flounced out of my room, and I wondered to myself with pursed lips just how much of my life wasn't how I'd always thought it was.

JESSI

When I walked into the kitchen, everyone had already heard the news and I could cut the atmosphere with a knife. I felt a bit self-conscious with all the looks I got as I made my way to my station.

"Um," I started nervously. "Hello?"

I waved at the others in the room, and they sent back half-hearted greetings as they turned back to their jobs, less lively than before.

"Sorry about that," the woman closest to me, Mary, leaned over to me to whisper. "Everyone just took the news hard."

I frowned. "What news?"

"That you're leaving," she clarified.

"Ah," I murmured, even though that didn't make any sense.

I'd been working with these people for a while, but besides Laura, I didn't talk to anyone much outside of work. And it wasn't like I was the only person who had come in and left, I'd just lasted longer. At least half the staff in the kitchen we either there when I arrived or had arrived at the same time I had. The remaining half came months after I was settled.

I didn't think they would even be attached to me.

My transfer had been approved already, even though it had only been a week. Usually, when someone was transferring, not just quitting, it took anytime between two weeks to a month. But I hadn't been bragging to Trent when I told him just how good I was. In my meeting with the manager, he'd told me that my talents would be appreciated wherever I ended up, and he was sad to see me go. I'd known he'd meant the words genuinely, not just as a polite send-off.

Days later, I got the news that one of the hotels out on the coast needed a pastry chef, and I was preparing to move.

Today was my last day at work, and the manager must have spread the word around. I would have preferred a quiet exit, but it did warm my heart just a little bit to realize I would at least be missed by my coworkers.

But really, a little beach time might be just what I needed to get my spirits up.

In the whole week, I'd managed to avoid Trent. I'd heard someone spread a rumor that he was looking for me, and I worked even harder to stay out of his way. I hadn't been back to my place for more than a few minutes for the past several days.

"Let's see," I muttered to myself. "What do I need to do for today…"

I was going to bake up a storm today, so the guys who occasionally helped me wouldn't have much to do in addition to their duties, but I could only make enough for today and tomorrow. More and I'd have to worry about some of the pastries and desserts going stale.

There was some lingering guilt for leaving on such short notice. The reason transfers had such a long timeline was so a replacement could be found in the meantime. If you were getting fired, chances were your replacement was already in waiting. And if you quit, then there was a scramble to find someone else. For such a big hotel chain, you'd think it would be easy, but with their high standards, even though plenty of people applied for jobs, actually getting one was rare.

As for me, I'd applied alongside more than fifty people, and I was the lucky girl to walk away with the job. Me and maybe three other guys.

But I was leaving them in a tough spot because I wanted to run away.

I was taking the coward's way out, and I did hate myself a little for it. It hadn't been easy to get through the hiring process to begin with, then I'd had to work hard to prove myself as a chef, to my colleagues in the kitchen and the management. In my time working at the hotel, I'd built up a rather nice nest egg in my bank account. In fact, the biggest hit it took since I got hired, was my parents' last anniversary gift and the two bottles of wine I'd recently replaced.

For the first time, I even had my own car. It was a second-hand car, unlike the ones lined up at the garage in the Thompson mansion, but I'd bought it with my own money and I'd been so proud. I had my own place, though it was at the hotel, and I paid my own bills.

I was a grown up. Somehow, Trent—in that talented way he had—easily turned me right back into that insecure teenage girl I used to be, even though I would be thirty in a few more years.

Damn you, Trent, I growled in my mind. Just... damn you!

Not that I could lay all the blame on him. I should have been avoiding him in the first place. And even though I was tipsy at the time, I never should have thrown myself at him like some desperate groupie.

That was a mistake.

I worked through the morning tirelessly, getting more done than I thought I would. There was still plenty to do, but I wanted to clock out early so I could go back to my room and finish packing.

Fuck, I thought to myself, as I dragged myself over to the staff room. I need to give a proper goodbye to my parents.

I'd stopped by the mansion and slept over a few times. Lucky for me, Trent wasn't there anymore, so there was no risk of me running into him. I hadn't explained to my parents how not only was I transferring, but I would be going far away. Mom just thought it was a trip, but she had no idea yet that the move could be more permanent. I'd run into Emily a couple of times as well, but we hadn't talked, so she also didn't know.

I didn't know how to tell any of them.

"Jessi!"

I looked up at the loud call with a wince. I wasn't the only person in the room, so I glared at Laura for her overly dramatic entrance. She didn't even seem to notice, rushing across the room and throwing herself into me with a loud squeal.

"The rumor's all over the place," she said, almost in a whine, as she nearly strangled me with her arms around my neck, rocking me from side to side a little too roughly. "Why are you going so far away?"

I tapped on her shoulder to get her to loosen her hold, then pulled away from her completely, shifting so I could put the length of the couch in between us.

"You knew I was leaving already," I told her wryly. Of course, she'd been the first person I'd told because I went back to her apartment for the second night. "What are people saying, anyway?"

"That you're going to some far away coast," she said quickly. "They make it sound like you're moving to a different country or something!"

I shrugged. "Laura, you already know I'm not."

"Well, yeah," she mumbled with a small pout. "But you're still going to be at a beach somewhere and we're not exactly close to one."

I shook my head. "Nope. We're a lot closer than you'd think. It's only about a six-hour drive away. It would be shorter by plane, but I'm moving with some of my things so I'll be driving."

"Why do you have to move at all?" she said with a sigh, finally settling down. The look she sent my way was curious and knowing at the same time. "I know it's about Trent, but what changed? Did something happen between the two of you? Because the last time we talked, I thought you'd just ignore him and be fine."

"That was the original plan," I said slowly.

I didn't want to tell her about him and me sleeping together, so I didn't say more than that.

She let out another sigh. I leaned back as she leaned closer to me, but she held her arms open instead of jumping me this time, and I reached for the hug.

"I'm going to miss you," she said wistfully. "Things are going to be so boring around here without you, and I know Emily will agree with me. I'll visit you sometime, okay?"

I nodded, unable to reply verbally because I was choked up, and I knew it was only the first round of goodbyes.

Why do I have to go anywhere?

As I got up to return to work, I went through all my memories of Trent. All the sweet ones, as few as they were, and the bad.

I thought back to before. When we were kids and still the closest friends, before and just after his mother died. We'd been best friends, as hard as it was to believe now. We'd played together a lot back then. Mainly because my parents were always working, I spent more hours out of the day with Trent since he was the only other child there at that time. His dad would have preferred if Trent went to his friends' houses and played with their kids, but his mom preferred to stay at home more often than not, and that was how we'd become close.

He was the sweetest little boy in those times. But then

his mom died, and he changed completely. The Trent I knew was gone, replaced with this sullen, reclusive kid who no longer wanted to play with me, even though he didn't always push me away. I figured if I stuck around long enough, he would go back to his former self.

Not that he did. Later, he became hurtful towards others and to me, even though I was the person who still hung around him the most.

Even through all of that, I'd never given up on him, never given up hope that one day I could get my best friend back, not even as I grew older and saw how cynical he was becoming.

But now, there was no helping it. I didn't like it, but I knew I had to face reality.

Trent was a jerk of the first order, and that probably wouldn't change. Those sunlit days of our forgotten youth were dead and gone, and now all that was left was me being unhappy and a man with a broken heart that would never heal because he would never let anyone try.

The way he touched me, though… I thought wistfully. Our one night together. The wonder of it all when it was all so new to me. How fascinated he'd looked as he'd ran his hands all over me. How almost vulnerable he'd been with absolutely no barriers between us for the first time in forever.

I sighed as the thoughts floated away because it had only been a moment. I'd been avoiding him, yeah, but he hadn't made much effort to see me besides asking here and there about my whereabouts. He probably hadn't meant for rumors to start, and I'd had my shifts all through the week, where I stayed put in one place. It wasn't like he hadn't found me, just hadn't put in too much effort past the first couple of days.

It was to be expected. I'd found news of him online without looking for it before. I'd seen pictures of the kind of women he usually had on his arm; expensive beauties that were so far out of my league I knew I would never stack up against them.

Yeah, I'd grown up, and I was shapely. Plenty of guys found me attractive enough to give a second look. But I didn't think I had it in me to be some rich man's ornament. Maybe, for Trent… if he had shown some more interest… but that night had obviously been some sort of lapse for him.

Just as it had been for me, I told myself forcefully.

It was time to leave. Time to cut him out of my heart.

15

TRENT

"Sir?" I heard the question as she knocked on my door. She didn't wait for me to reply as I sighed and looked up.

"Yes?"

The secretary walked in, a folder held in her arm, and I knew it was just one more thing for me to do. I'd migrated recently from working with hard copy documents, thanks in large part to my brothers, who were now off somewhere supposedly attending to their 'duties.' I was still waiting for news that Mason had thrown a party somewhere. Kevin would be more circumspect, but I'd probably hear something about him too.

Occasionally there'd be something for me to look into, which meant I had to stop whatever else I was doing to get to it because all the late arrivals were super fucking important, and I couldn't put them off.

"I have some new documents for you to look over... but

if you don't have time, sir...?" she started slowly, and I could have pushed her away but I knew that it had to be done.

"It's fine," I said, cutting her off. "Please set it down. How soon do you need it back?"

"An hour. It needs at least three signatures."

I sighed. So, it was probably a contract or something. Were Dad's business partners changing the rules of the game now that the old man was out of commission for the time being? I needed to find the original if there was one, then read through the whole document and decide whether to sign or not, or send it back and wait for it to be returned...

I'd be happier if it were just something to do from within the hotel, but I'd taken care of all of those already. My secretary made sure.

"You'll have it. Come back for it in exactly one hour." I waved my hand from side-to-side trying to gauge how long it would take me to sort it out.

"Yes, sir," she said with a nod, then turned and walked out the office.

As soon as she was gone, I dropped my head into my arms. What I wanted to do was knock my head on the desk, but the last thing I needed was to give myself a headache anyway.

"Where did my free time go, exactly?" I muttered to myself, starting to feel resentment at my lack of spare time.

Sure, I was used to working for days on end with no breaks, it wasn't exactly a new thing to me. The problem was it had been a fucking week already, and because I was so bogged down with work, I hadn't had the time to properly track Jessi down for that talk. I was taking too damn long to find her, and I was worried how her thoughts would have changed over the course of that time.

On the other hand, I'd had a lot of time to think about her. Even when I was working, thoughts of Jessi tended to intrude on my mind to the point that I was growing used to it. Besides thinking about her, I also had a lot of time to examine my own life.

I'd managed to come to the conclusion I lacked something in my life. And what could it possibly be, besides that one thing that had settled in my head and refused to leave for the past week?

My life had been lacking Jessi. It wasn't an easy conclusion to make, but it was one that made sense to me after the week I'd had of dreaming and daydreaming about her.

Focus, I thought to myself. The day isn't over yet.

I got started reading the new document. As if to mock me, my phone rang. I winced when I saw it was a call from my PA back in Asheville. It had been easy before, to help out with Dad's empire when I was still working on my own company, but now that I was fully focused on both, I was starting to feel the strain.

I managed to do a quick read of the document as I listened to my PA, and by the end of the hour when the secretary came for it, I handed the signed document over. I was getting back to what I'd been doing before, only for my phone to ring again. I had to pick it up, and it was nearly a whole hour of chatting over the phone so I could help fix a situation on the other end.

After a few more minutes of working, my phone rang again. Only, it wasn't my PA this time. I vaguely remembered it as some woman's number. I'd probably given her my number at some party, and she was calling because I hadn't made the first move.

Dammit. Can't you people just leave me alone? I'm busy!

I was almost to the point of tearing my hair out. I rejected the call, but she called back a minute later. I let out a low growl, then sighed.

"I'm taking a break," I declared to my empty office, glaring at my phone as I picked it up and turned it off. Then I turned to the computer and logged out of the hotel's database before turning it off. I got up, pulled on my jacket, and left.

The secretary looked up as I walked out of the office, surprised. I didn't blame her. I might have only been at my dad's office for a week, but this was the earliest I'd ever come out of it.

"Sir?" she said, a slight frown of confusion on her brow.

"I'm taking a break," I told her. "If anything comes up, please take care of it for me. I'll be completely out of communication for the rest of today, but I'll be back tomorrow. I have something important to take care of."

"Yes, sir."

Good.

I all but strutted down the hall to the elevator, feeling total relief to be free of obligation for a few hours. Jessi's shift should have ended already, so it should be easy to track her down. Hopefully.

Once the elevator doors closed between me and the hallway, I pulled out a piece of paper I'd been keeping with me since I'd had the secretary look into Jessi for me. It was her complete schedule and the number of the room where she was staying.

I went to her quarters first, deciding I'd go looking for her down in the staff room or the kitchens if I didn't find her there today. I wondered idly where she'd been staying when she wasn't at home, and if I should be worried she was finally looking for some new guy.

The thought didn't sit well with me.

At her door, I paused before knocking. I'd come here over the past week, only to go back when there was no reply to my knocking. I didn't want the same to happen today, even though I had more determination, and more time, to properly track her down this time.

I'd never been on the inside of her room, but being the owner had a few perks. I knew her place was little more than a living room, bathroom, and bedroom. There was a tiny area to cook in, but it wasn't really impressive. Her place was about half the size of mine at the hotel. My kitchen area was bigger, not that I used it to cook much.

After some minutes to muster up some courage, I knocked on the door, then held my breath as I waited. To my complete surprise, the door opened, and Jessi stood on the other side of it. She was just as surprised to see me, and we stood there for a minute, staring at each other.

"Um, hi," I said after a minute, my eyes drifting away

from hers. I noticed she had a lot of boxes in the apartment, and my eyebrows shot up. "Are you moving or something?" I asked, joking. "Or is the room so small it's the only way you can store your things?"

Either she wasn't into humor, or my brand of humor was terrible because her expression didn't change at all. It was probably the latter, but I clued in that she was acting particularly serious. There was a slight frown on her face as she looked up at me, and I couldn't help but mirror it.

"What?" I said defensively. Was she mad at me after all?

"It's true," she said.

It took me a minute to understand what she meant. And then I was shocked again.

"You're leaving?" I blurted out. "Why?"

She arched an eyebrow, giving me a strange look.

That was a stupid question, I thought to myself. Fuck. Could there be any other reason? Jessi wants to leave because of me.

"Stay." I winced, wondering where I was getting this urge to start blurting shit out. I didn't take it back. "You don't have to go anywhere," I continued. "Just stay at the hotel. If the place is too small, I can find someplace bigger for you to stay, something with a better kitchen. You've been working here long enough that you deserve it, anyway."

Words were falling out of my mouth, words I didn't have the time to think on before blurting them out. Jessi's expression had fallen blank in shock, but I couldn't stop. I needed to stop her from leaving, whatever the means, even if it meant making a fool of myself. I didn't understand the sudden panic, or where it came from. I couldn't let Jessi leave.

"About what you said before, you being a good chef? I agree. The hotel needs you here, so there's no need for you to go anywhere. Would you like a raise? I can approve it if you go through the proper channels, trust me when I say you'd deserve it. I've had some of your creations over the past several days. They're some of the best I've tasted, Jessi, and I get around."

I knew I was going to regret this at some point. After the way I'd been treating her over the years, I was suddenly singing her praises. Shit, I hadn't even apologized for how I talked to her the last time yet! I had a lot to be sorry for where she was concerned. At the very least, I should have snuck in a sorry in there.

"Trent."

All she did was say my name, but it was enough to get me to stop, just short of blurting out that apology. I sucked in a sharp breath, surprised that I hadn't been taking breaths in between all that talking. The expression on Jessi's face had changed, though I couldn't understand what she was thinking.

Then, Jessi took a step closer to me. And then another, followed by another, closing the space between us. I watched her, suddenly fascinated with what she planned on doing.

When she stopped right in front of me and rose up on her tiptoe, it was like instinct for me to duck my head lower, so she could press her lips to mine. The kiss started out soft, chaste, just a press of lips. It was reminiscent of our first kiss from back in our teen years.

I let out a low groan, my arms slipping around her waist to hold her body to mine. I nipped, then licked her lips until she parted them for me, and I deepened the kiss. She gave a breathy moan that had shivers running up and down my spine, and my cock growing hard in my slacks.

"Jessi," I gasped her name when I pulled back after a minute.

She was looking up at me; eyes still closed, lips flushed a dark pink from the kiss, a light blush on her cheeks. She opened her eyes slowly to meet mine, and the heat in them made my body light up.

Fuck.

I realized, belatedly, that we were still in the hallway. I didn't care if someone saw us kiss, but I wouldn't let them see more. I walked Jessi backward into her apartment, and she went with it, her arms sliding up over my arms, my shoulders, then circling my neck as she clung to me. Once inside, I closed the door behind us, turned us around, and pushed her against the door.

"I want you, Jessi," I admitted, my voice coming out low and husky. She should know just how badly I wanted her, so much more than I'd ever wanted anyone. I found I had a problem then, I couldn't find the words to explain it.

"I want you, too, Trent," Jessi said in a whisper.

The admission was enough to get me to forget everything else. I ducked my head down to ravage her mouth in a kiss, reaching for her clothes to pull them off.

Right then, I wanted her in bed, under me, and I wanted

it as fast as possible. Jessi didn't seem to mind, moaning into the kiss as her own hands pushed my coat off my shoulders, then fumbled for the buttons of my shirt.

I chuckled into the kiss, keeping one arm tight around her waist as I kissed her hard.

You're mine, Jessi. For tonight, and hopefully, for many more nights to come.

16

JESSI

*W*hy is this happening again?

The thought entered my mind, and just as quickly was swept away with more kisses as Trent held me tightly as if he would never let me go. I knew better than to read too much into the gesture. We were both getting caught up in the moment again. I knew once it was gone I would regret it.

But how could I not jump him again after he said all that!

To say it was a surprise would be a major understatement. The man who could never seem to run out of ways to insult me and belittle me was suddenly speaking up in my favor. It made no sense, and I didn't know his motivation, but I couldn't deny that I was moved. And then it hit me again.

I was moving. Moving somewhere not too far, but far enough that I wouldn't be able to run into anyone I knew by coincidence. There would be no seeing my friends and family every day. There would be no seeing Trent.

And yet, he'd shown up in front of me. This was my one last chance with him, after this, we'd never get to see each other again. When I thought that, I couldn't help but want one last go-round with the love of my life before I threw all of that behind me.

In spite of his asking me to stay… my plan was to leave, and nothing would change that.

"Let's go to the bedroom," I said in between kisses, starting to feel the urgency. Not just my impending departure; I remembered the last time we did this and how good it felt. I was in a hurry to have that feeling back.

After one last hard kiss, Trent pulled back to grin down at me.

"Lead the way," he said, releasing all of me but my hand.

I bit my lip and stared at his face, trying to memorize it. There hadn't been time for me to see it properly before, and the alcohol hadn't helped. But now I could see it, Trent looking at me like he was happy to look at me for once, not like I was something scraped out from the tread of his expensive designer shoes.

It was a lovely sight.

"Is something wrong, Jessi?" he asked, his voice gentle. He tucked a stray lock of hair behind my ear.

My breath blew out of me in a heavy gust, and I did my best not to show too much surprise. What would I do, if he realized what he was doing and decided it was a mistake? If he suddenly did a one-eighty on me and became the asshole from before?

I couldn't handle that, not now. Not when I was about to get exactly what I wanted.

This time, I even came prepared. I'd hoped he would come by to see me, and it had seemed like a vain hope the more I packed and he still hadn't shown up. I had some condoms on the nightstand in my bedroom waiting for us. It was easier than taking another pill, and I couldn't just take one on the off chance he would come looking for me.

The condoms made me seem just a little less desperate. If he wondered why I had them in the first place… I was going to lie like my life depended on it. I wasn't sure what lie to tell just yet, if he even asked, but I would have one to give.

"The bedroom," I muttered, after long moments of memorizing his face, and he didn't once interrupt me as he looked me over himself, still with that gentle look that I wasn't used to receiving from him. "It's this way."

I squeezed his hand where it lay in mine, then turned and led the way. It was a short trip, but we had to walk around the boxes to get there.

"You don't have a lot of stuff," Trent muttered, probably to himself, but I heard him anyway.

"Yeah, well. We don't all have the kind of background you do. I don't have a lot of stuff to my name."

All the stuff I had was already packed away in the boxes, and it was just enough that I could fit it all into my car if I used the trunk and the backseat. The only stuff I had left out was my outfit for tomorrow and the bedding because I wouldn't be leaving until the morning.

I will be leaving, I promised myself. Once it's morning, everything is over. But just one more time…

Trent turned me around once we got into the bedroom, and I let him walk me backward to the bed. He didn't break his gaze once, and I could feel my heart start to beat fast and hard in my chest as my excitement grew. As much as I'd tried to make myself stop thinking about our first time, I couldn't, and I wanted tonight to be just as good, if not better.

"You're something, you know that," Trent murmured, finally coming to a stop. The hand still holding mine released it, only to wrap back around my waist and tug my body against his. "You grew up beautiful, Jessi."

I pursed my lips, feeling my cheeks warm with a blush. Don't listen to him, Jessi! It's a trick!

"You're just saying that," I accused.

He smiled crookedly at me. "Believe what you want. I could always show you what you do to me?"

It was worded as a question, but I wasn't given time to answer. He ducked his head and I sighed into his kiss, standing on tiptoes to kiss him back, my hands sliding over his shoulders again. His coat was gone from when we'd first embraced out in the front room, so he was left in just his shirt. I'd undone a few of the buttons but had forgotten the tie because it was still there around his neck.

I took my time, mapping the inside of his mouth. I didn't know quite what I was doing since Trent was the only man I'd ever kissed. But I tried to call on what I'd learned from last time. I licked his lip to gain access, then tentatively slid my tongue into his mouth, licking the roof of his mouth, then tangling our tongues together. Trent sucked on my tongue, and I moaned as I held myself even closer to him.

Focus, Jessi. Get to the bed first…

My arms moved around his neck until my hands were at his collar, and I went to work on his tie. It came loose with a couple of tugs, then I was working on his buttons. It was going a little slow because he kept distracting me with kisses, but I did manage to get all the way to where his shirt was tucked into his pants. I tugged it out, finished unbuttoning, and then pushed it off his shoulders.

I groaned when he stopped kissing me to pull it off when I'd managed to avoid it so far. He chuckled at me. With his shirt off, he undid his belt and my lips parted as I watched him slowly strip down in front of me. He paused with his fly undone, and when I met his gaze he had an eyebrow arched my way.

"I'm not going to be the only one getting naked, am I?" he asked cheekily, adding a little grin.

"You're in an unusually good mood today," I muttered with a pout. I reached around my back to pull down my zip, realizing just then that he'd already pulled it more than halfway down already. I finished pulling it down, then wrapped my arms around myself, hands on my shoulders, trying to talk myself into actually taking it off.

This is the worst kind of time to start feeling shy, I chided myself. But Trent staring at me so intently wasn't exactly helping.

"I have been looking for you for the whole week," he admitted. "Well, trying, anyway. I was too busy. I came here the day after we were together last time, but I didn't see you."

That had me stilling in shock, but in the next moment, I was dismissing it in my mind. It couldn't possibly mean anything. Trent looked so beautiful, so sincere in that moment, but how could I take his word for it? There was no way it could be true.

Leopards didn't change their spots, after all, and especially not so quickly that it would give me whiplash if I wasn't already planning on running away, so I didn't see him go back to his usual self.

I was giving myself this one last chance. So I could feel the way he'd made me feel that night one last time.

"Are you just going to stand there?" I snapped after a moment of neither of us moving.

Trent smirked and let his pants drop, kicking them to the side. My jaw dropped at how readily he did it, though he still had his briefs on. Steeling myself, I slid the dress off my shoulders and kicked it to the side as well. I stood in front of him, half naked, wanting to cover myself with my hands, but holding back the urge.

"So beautiful," Trent murmured, closing the space between us again and taking me in his arms as he pressed our lips together for another kiss.

We tumbled into the bed. My bed wasn't as big or as soft as Trent's bed. If we rolled around too much, one of us would probably end up on the floor. He didn't seem to mind, holding me close as he settled right in the middle. I shoved at his briefs as he undid my bra, and we stripped our underwear off, tossing them to the floor.

"Nightstand," I gasped out before he could push me down again. "My nightstand, first drawer."

Trent grumbled but leaned over to reach for the drawer. I lowered myself onto my back and waited. He pulled out the condoms and arched an eyebrow down at me. He didn't say anything though, kneeing my thighs apart and settling between my legs. I bit down on my lower lip as I watched him open up the condom and slide the rubber onto his cock. I'd never seen a man naked like this. The last time didn't count because I didn't remember seeing it. I wasn't a virgin anymore, but seeing how big he was, I was suddenly hit with the same fear from that night.

I forgot it pretty quickly because Trent knew just what he was doing. He caught my legs under the knees to wrap them around his hips, then leaned down, so his upper body lay above mine. One arm wrapped around my waist, arching my back slightly as he pressed licks and kisses all over my breasts. I gasped and moaned every time he flicked my nipple or wrapped his lips around one and sucked.

He had me squirming and writhing under him in seconds, keeping me distracted so I didn't even have time to feel fear when his cock slid into me. He was far gentler than before, and it still felt just as good.

"Trent," I moaned out, tipping my head back as I swiveled my hips, gasping at the feel of being so full. "Please, move."

He hummed, his lips moving from my chest as he kissed up my neck. His hips moved, slowly at first, pulling back until just the tip of him remained inside me, then entering me in a slow thrust. He started up a rhythm, adding a roll to his hips with every thrust. I dug my fingers into his shoulders as I held on, my legs tight around his hips.

"Jessi," he whispered.

My eyes fluttered open at the call of my name, and I met his gaze. There was this unreadable look in them, but before I could decipher it, he was kissing me. His hips moved faster until his hips slammed into mine with every thrust as he fucked me into the mattress. My moans and cries were muffled in his kisses, and he sneaked a hand between us to cup one of my breasts, his thumb and fore-finger teasing the nipple.

Pleasure pooled at the base of my spine, and I broke away from the kiss, tipping my head back. He moved to kissing all over my neck, the arm around my waist holding tightly onto my hip, and I knew I would have marks to carry with me for a few days.

"Trent!"

I cried out his name as my body started to shiver. I dragged my nails down his back, and he growled as we hit the climax. Trent's hips stilled against mine, and I could feel him pulse inside me as I convulsed hard around his cock.

We slumped into the bed, sated, and Trent rolled us to the side, keeping me in his arms. I held onto him just as tightly, closing my eyes and burying my face into his chest as a stray tear leaked out of my eye.

Goodbye, Trent. I don't want to, but I'm sure I'll miss you.

17

TRENT

I held Jessi close, feeling her holding me just as tightly.

What am I doing?

The thought kept running through my mind as I realized this wasn't exactly normal behavior for me. Of all the women I'd had sex with, I didn't usually end up asleep in the same bed with them, and even in the few cases I did, there was never this... *cuddling* afterward.

I realized I really loved feeling her soft, smaller body pressed against me.

"Jessi?" I called tentatively.

There was no answer. She squirmed a little and curled further into my chest, and I couldn't help grinning.

I am never letting you go again, Jessi, I thought to myself with determination.

It felt more like admitting something I'd known for a while than coming to a realization that she was really important to me. Besides, I'd practically bared my soul to her twice now. I wasn't sure if she knew how important it was that I'd let my walls down around her. After that, I just couldn't let her go.

My body shivered a little as I ducked my head into her hair and breathed deeply. Jessi was still asleep in my arms. I'd never done this before with my bed partners, but for Jessi, I could allow a lot. I knew, for her, I could let myself start to love again. It was something so foreign to me, but I knew it would come so easily with Jessi by my side.

I wasn't sure when I fell asleep. I didn't think I could, feeling so giddy for the first time in a long while. But I did eventually drift off, dreaming of Jessi as I held her close in my arms. My dreams were all about our past, present, and future. I hadn't forgotten how she was the closest person to me before my mom died. I'd pushed everyone away, but Jessi had always stuck around. I hadn't been nice to her back then, but now I could feel the ice around my heart start to melt.

As for our future... I hoped we had one together, anyway. It would be just perfect if that dream could come true.

Then, I woke up, and once again, I was alone.

Really Jessi? I thought with a frown. Why did she keep doing that? I stretched out then moved to where I'd dropped my clothes, searching for my phone through them. It wasn't that early in the morning, so maybe she was just at work?

That's right, I thought to myself, feeling placated. There wasn't anything else that would get her out of bed early, right? She had her obligations to the hotel. She probably got up early to head to work.

I got dressed in yesterday's clothes, leaving my shirt only partway buttoned and leaving off the tie. I didn't look around the room as I left, though I couldn't help but notice the boxes she'd had around were all gone.

"She probably just put the stuff back," I said to myself in reassurance.

She had a long shift usually, and I couldn't go down to bother her. Besides, that would only fuel the rumors, and I needed to kill them before they grew even more annoying.

It was early enough that I didn't worry about anyone catching me coming out of her room. I rushed back to mine to jump into the shower. I hummed as I stood under the warm spray, keeping the shower short. Then I was getting dressed for my day. I left my room and headed for the elevators to take me up to the office.

I was tempted to give Jessi a call. Then I remembered she hadn't officially given me her number yet. It was still there in the records, but I couldn't bring myself to use that. The elevator doors opened before I could think too much about it, and I stepped outside.

Besides, I would probably only be a bother to her. Jessi had always been the responsible type, and if I tried to butt in while she was working she would be annoyed with me. Besides, it was one of the reasons I admired her so much. She knew what needed to be done and she went and did it. As much as my dad had tried to teach me, I'd learned that sort of attitude from her.

"Good morning, sir."

I stopped with a blink because I'd almost just walked past the secretary. Usually, I greeted her in the morning. If she hadn't called out to me, I would have forgotten.

I gave her a wide grin as I said, "Good morning to you too. Have some coffee sent up for me before starting anything, all right? Thank you."

She was left stunned as I walked into the office. And while I knew why, I didn't care.

I was happy.

The realization was a pretty obvious one, but I couldn't help grinning at the thought. For the first time in a long time, I could say I was genuinely happy, and it was all because of Jessi. My day was better because I was thinking of when I would get to see her later.

My coffee came in twenty minutes later, and I thanked both the server and the secretary as she'd let him in. I was left to myself, humming as I drank my coffee and logged into my computer. I picked up work where I'd left off yesterday, feeling more excited than I'd felt in a long while to get to work.

After a while, I picked up my phone because I couldn't help myself. I had Jessi's number, so why not use it? I sent a quick text.

Hey, Jessi. It's me, Trent. Let me know if you got into work okay.

I winced because it was the best I could think of, but I felt like I could have done better. I put my phone down, but even as I went back to work I kept eyeing my phone, waiting for a reply. None came for a while, then a knock on the door diverted my attention.

"Come in," I called, leaning back in my chair.

The secretary walked in, followed by my brothers. I grinned.

"Mason, Kevin! Aren't you guys up a little early? I figured you both like to sleep in."

Both my brothers froze, but the secretary crossed the room, picked up the mug, and walked away without a word. She closed the door behind herself, and the noise seemed to jolt my brothers, because they approached the desk again.

"Did something happen to you?" Mason asked, eyes slightly narrowed.

I didn't want them to know. I didn't want anyone to know, but it wasn't exactly easy to hide when I wanted to burst out into song, as ridiculous as it would be. I was happy, but I didn't need to broadcast it, especially to my suspicious-as-fuck brothers. I checked myself, rearranging my expression into something blank. I had to keep to my usual routine, and the usual me was always serious and polite, not grinning at everyone.

I was happy. Really, truly happy for the first time in a long while.

"Nothing happened," I said, waving away his suspicions, though I couldn't help a slight twitch of my lips. "But I would like to hear from you guys. You've supposedly been working. Do you have anything to show for it?"

That got them to start fidgeting, and I smirked. It was different from a grin, and I did it often so this one was allowed.

"What about you, Kevin?" I asked.

He frowned. "We have actually been working. If you want anything physical to show for it, you're going to have to wait. It's only been a few days."

I sighed, shaking my head in mock disappointment. "Really, boys. I know I'm the oldest here, but I can't keep supervising you. I will if it's the only way to get you to do shit, though, so why don't I have the desks brought back in here, huh?"

Mason immediately shook his head. "Dude, no way! Work is so much more than just sitting behind a desk all day, you know? You can just keep doing that while we take care of everything else."

I sighed. "That isn't really fair to me though, is it? I feel like I'm doing all the work." I pursed my lips. "I guess I have to admit I'm impressed. I haven't heard any news of you hosting a party yet."

His eyes drifted away from mine as he looked shifty.

"Well, about that…"

I snorted. "No way. You actually have one planned, don't you?" I turned to Kevin. "What about you?"

He raised his hands, palms out, and backed away slowly. "Do not look at me like that, I swear I'm not planning anything. Besides, I'd probably just step out for a walk instead of inconveniencing the hotel staff."

"Why is it an inconvenience?" Mason countered. "It's their jobs, isn't it? And it's not like I wouldn't pay just because I'm the son of the owner!"

I held in my snickers as I watched them bicker between themselves. It was just like Mason to have a party planned. I'd known, but having the confirmation didn't leave me as annoyed as I'd thought it would. Mason would always be Mason, after all. If he didn't have the party at the hotel, I knew he'd go somewhere else to bother other people.

Kevin would probably get himself lost exploring. But this was our hometown, so I'd have to hope he wouldn't actually get himself lost. Besides, these two weren't kids I was supposed to babysit. We were all chipping in to help in our own way. I knew they were doing something for the hotel, even if I didn't know what it was yet.

"You can have your party," I cut into their bickering, and they turned to me with twin expressions of surprise. "But there have to be a few ground rules. You know you can't bother other guests when you do have your party, right? If you do, I swear I will kick you out."

"Of course I wouldn't," Mason said indignantly, even as he still watched me in surprise.

I gave a sharp nod. "The other condition is you absolutely have to give me a heads up before this thing happens. I don't think I'll be making an appearance, but I know I'll be getting calls for it once you set this party up, and I'd like to be prepared for it."

They both stared at me for a moment, then shared a look between themselves.

"Something definitely happened," Mason declared. "But you know what? I don't care what it is. I'll let you know before I start throwing any parties, and you don't have to worry, they won't be too wild."

Both Kevin and I scoffed at that, and Mason put on a betrayed look. It was hard to believe him because of all the outrageous stories I'd heard. A lot of it was probably exaggeration, but I'd stopped going to his parties after the first few I was pushed into attending for a reason.

After some more brotherly bickering, they left and I went back to work. Only to pause and pick up my phone.

Finally, after years, I was feeling happy. It was all because of Jessi.

So where was she?

Probably just busy, I told myself, writing her another quick text to get back to me when she could. I promised myself I'd look for her later.

With that decided, I put the phone down and turned to my computer, ready to focus. I had several hours before I could see her and I had to make them count.

18

JESSI

I woke up for the second time wrapped in Trent's arms.

Why can't I just stay like this?

The thought was a wistful one because I knew all the reasons why not. I wasn't just going to disregard them, thinking things could possibly work out. There was nothing to stake that kind of faith and hope on, after all.

Still, I gave myself a few minutes to enjoy being held like this. As far as I cared, Trent was the man for me. Once I left, I wasn't sure I would ever look at someone else the way I looked at him. So, arguably, this was my last chance to get in some snuggling.

After several minutes, during which my mind woke up, I sighed, knowing I had to get going. It was early because my work schedule had pretty much been ingrained in me. Today, had I still been going to work, I would have been going in for the early morning shift. Someone else would have to take my place by now.

"I'm sorry, Trent," I whispered, blinking tears away. I placed a soft kiss on his chest, then got out of bed carefully.

I needed a shower and a change of clothes, and I did those listlessly, even as I tried to be quiet so I wouldn't disturb him. It would just be more difficult if he woke up, and I had to explain to him that I was leaving anyway, even after he'd asked me to stay.

Once he wakes up and I'm not there, he'll realize this was for the best, I told myself.

That was what I was hoping for. I hoped he wouldn't be too annoyed with me for leaving. Who was I kidding? He probably wouldn't even care that much.

"I need to get this stuff out," I muttered to myself once I was dressed, my hands on my hips as I looked at the disorganized mess that was my living room. I packed away my clothes from yesterday, picking up Trent's and leaving them on top of my dresser. Then I packed away my toiletries and sighed. "Now for the move to the car."

I started with moving the boxes. I was so glad I'd already sent a few outside because this was going to be a tedious process.

I picked them up one by one and left them outside the door. Once I had everything outside, I closed the door behind me. It was early enough that I wouldn't have to worry about anybody coming by and taking my things if I left them alone for a little bit.

I carried them one by one over to the elevator. I checked to see if it was in working order first, then moved the rest of the boxes to the outside of the elevator. Once I had them all, I pressed the button to head down, and when the elevator doors opened, I pushed all my stuff inside. I had to put one of the boxes in the way of the door when it was about to close early, but I finally got everything inside. I breathed another sigh and waited until I got down.

The process repeated, with me pushing the stuff out, leaving them on the outside of the elevator, then taking them one by one to my car, waiting outside in the staff parking.

After half an hour, I was ready to leave. And I did, jumping into the front of the car and putting it in drive. There were plenty of people I would have liked to have seen before I left, but they likely wouldn't have been awake.

I drove out of the parking lot, easing the car into the street, then picking up speed. I knew the general direction I was supposed to be heading. I wasn't sure how long I'd been driving when I lost the fight with my emotions and tears started streaming down my face as I cried silently. Familiar streets and buildings fell away behind me the further I went, until I was out of town, and there was nothing but a long stretch road ahead, and fields of grass to either side.

My phone rang. It made me jump but my hands on the wheel remained steady. I glanced over at my phone, checking the screen and seeing the name on it. I grimaced.

Emily.

I hadn't exactly been avoiding her along with Trent, but she and I hadn't really met up since he'd showed. I hadn't talked to her either, and I wondered if she even knew what was happening. She hadn't been to the hotel since her father got sick and her brothers came back.

She would be annoyed with me if I didn't answer, so I used my hands-free feature to pick up her call.

"Hi, Jessi," came her usually chipper voice, though I could hear some slight strain in it. "Sorry I haven't gotten in touch, things are a bit hectic over here."

"That's fine," I said quickly in reassurance. "I should have tried to call you first. My mom told me as much as she knew but I wanted to ask how your dad was doing."

There was a short silence. "Dad is… doing just fine. He's resting."

I let out a sigh of relief and nodded even though she couldn't see it. I'd been a little worried that what happened to Matthew Thompson was serious because it was so unlike him to not work. Even when he'd supposedly retired, my mom and I had known it was an excuse to stay at the mansion instead of traveling all over the place, but he still worked from home and at the hotel branch nearest to him.

"That's not what I called about," she said hurriedly. "I wanted to talk to you about Trent."

I wondered whether or not I should be surprised.

"You know about him and me?" I asked.

She sighed. "Well, I didn't at first. You mom certainly doesn't know." The words were accusing, and I winced. "But I heard the rumors. I don't know how much of it is true, but… my brother played with you, didn't he?"

I pursed my lips at the wording. "First of all, never say

that. You can't call what went down between me and Trent 'play', Emily. I don't know what you've heard, but it's true that I've been in love with Trent for a long time, and… we clashed when he came back."

Emily hummed. "It was a bit of a surprise when he suddenly started looking for me. Usually, he wouldn't give me the time of day. And then I show up on his doorstep, and he's asking me all about you. I was worried, Jessi."

"There was no need for you to worry."

"But something happened, didn't it? I'm not going to ask what… but there was something?"

I couldn't answer her. I wiped my tears away as they blurred my eyesight, but I could feel my throat tightening uncomfortably. I was far from done with crying.

"Where are you right now?" she asked.

I sighed, knowing she probably heard the news that I was leaving, too.

"I'm sorry," I said first thing. "I should have told you first when I was going to leave. You're right. Something did happen between me and Trent."

"Was it enough to make you run away?"

I shook my head. "I couldn't stay there, Emily. I just… couldn't stay close to him after everything. I'm already in too deep, and I know him. He might not be outright plotting it, but he's going to break my heart if I stay, I just know it. He's already done it so many times without trying, this wouldn't be any different."

Except it might be, I thought.

I pushed that thought away, or I wouldn't have made

the decision to run away. I'd pretty much bared all of myself to this man. There was no way I could handle any disappointment from him after that.

"Couldn't you try to stick around and work things out though?" Emily reasoned. "I mean… you probably know my big brother better than I do, but he can't be that big of an ass, right?"

I huffed a small laugh. "I don't know about that. I mean, he's changed over the years since I've known him, but there are parts that are familiar. I might know him better but it's not by much. But he… started making promises this time, and that's probably the scariest part. I know they're not things he can give me."

There was a short silence, and I wondered what Emily was thinking. My own thoughts were replaying last night, from when Trent showed up at my door and asked me to stay, then started giving out praises like he actually believed everything he was saying. It… all had to be a lie, right?

"I see," Emily finally said, her voice tight. "And there's absolutely no way for you to change your mind?"

I shook my head slowly. "I don't think that would be possible at this point, Emily. I'm sorry I didn't talk to you about any of this before."

"It's fine, I understand," she said. "He's my brother, of course it would be awkward for you to speak to me about him. As much as I don't like this, I wish you luck, Jessi. Keep in touch, okay?"

"Thanks, and you too."

With that, we hung up. I wiped away the fresh tears, took a deep breath, and drove on.

My destination was Myrtle Beach, and it was a six-hour drive to the new hotel I'd be working at. I just wanted to get there and start getting settled in. I wasn't sure about a lot of things, like where I would stay and what my position there would be in the kitchens, because there was always some hierarchy. But right then, I just wanted to get out of the car.

I had a week. When the manager told me, I'd wanted to let him know that I wouldn't need it, but I got it anyway. I would have a week to change my mind, if I wanted to stay at the new hotel or go back to Charlotte, but I doubted I would.

As abrupt as it was, I knew I needed this change. And besides, after I'd set it all up, it was too late to change my mind, wasn't it? What would be there for me to go back to anyway, now that I'd actually left? Trent would be annoyed with me after I stole away for a second time while he slept. It would do me no good.

Even if Emily said I could change my mind, there was no point now. With all the rumors I'd left behind, I could just imagine what the staff would come up with if I suddenly came back after a transfer. And even if I was making a mistake, it was made. If I went back and Trent ripped into me for it, I couldn't take that any more than him not keeping the promises he'd made to me.

You're doing the right thing, I told myself. It was the only thing I could have done in the situation I was left in.

I truly believed that. But... why did I keep looking in

the rearview mirror? There was no way someone would be coming after me to stop me, to get me to go back. I knew that logically, but the further I got from my hometown, the more my heart dropped.

It was my fault for having expectations. It's time to move on… to my new, boring life.

19

———

TRENT

It was just about lunch, and I'd paused working for the time being. After a moment of sitting back with my eyes closed to relax, I sat up and reached for my phone.

Still nothing.

How busy could she be that she wouldn't even reply to my texts? Or was she going to go back to ignoring me, as she had before? Even after last night? I'd thought things would be different, but was it just me?

Fuck, I thought to myself as I came to a realization. I am such an idiot.

How exactly were things supposed to change for the better between us? I hadn't even talked to her about things yet.

I need to talk to her, I decided. Right now.

I didn't know if she'd be on her break or not, or if she would still be in the kitchens. But I decided to give it a try, and picked up my phone to call her. I would have to come

183

up with an excuse for how I got her number. Considering how prickly I knew she could be, it would be less weird if I asked someone for her number than if I got it using my standing in the company.

Before I could dial the number, the door opened with enough force to slam it against the wall, making me look up. I was surprised to note my unexpected visitor was my half-sister.

"Emily," I said, putting my phone down. "What the hell are you doing here?"

"Trent."

The way she said my name made me look at her a little more closely, and I only then noticed how she was trembling. She had her hands fisted at her sides, her eyes were narrowed at me, and her lips were pressed flat.

"You look livid," I muttered. "What's wrong with you? Did something happen with Dad?"

She growled at me, and it was shocking enough that my eyes widened. I was pretty good at keeping my composure around other people in most situations, but I was caught off guard right then.

"Why the fuck are you still sitting on your ass, huh? Get up! You've got places you need to be."

I arched an eyebrow at her. "What are you talking about?" I said. "I still have plenty of work to do here—"

She cut me off by crossing the space between us and slamming her fists down on my desk. The force of it was enough to make a loud sound that made me jump. I tried to play it off as I shrugged, even though she didn't look like she cared in the least that I was a bit ruffled by her behavior. I glanced down at her hands, wondering if she felt okay after slamming them so hard, but I figured she would snap at me if I asked, so I kept my mouth shut. My little sister was just a tad bit angry.

"You are going to get Jessi back," she outright demanded.

I blinked, not understanding. "I'm sorry?"

"You will get your ass on the family helicopter," she said through gritted teeth. "You will go and retrieve my friend, big brother, and you will bring her back. I know you probably don't understand because you have a black heart, but she is the closest thing I have to a best friend."

"I didn't know the two of you were so close," I said tentatively. What was she on about anyway? Get Jessi from where exactly?

She let out a sigh, her whole body shuddering as the air passed between her lips. Her head ducked down, and she stayed in that position, bent over my desk, for a moment. When she stood up, she looked a bit calmer than before. She removed her hands, shaking them out, then flipping a lock of hair back over her shoulder.

"There's something going on between you and Jessi, isn't there? And don't even pretend you don't know who I'm talking about right now, Trent, because if you try, I will hit you." From the steel in her gaze, I knew she meant it. She was not playing around. I backed away from her a little.

"I know the Jessi you're talking about." I frowned at her, just slightly, smoothing a hand down the front of my shirt as I finally found my composure again. "If you're asking whether there is anything between Jessi and me, then yes. It's none of your business though."

She scoffed, giving me the stink eye. "It is my business if just your mere presence sends my friend packing, big brother."

The words were said derisively, but I hardly cared, because her words had just sunk in for me. And my composure was gone again as I looked up at her with shock.

Jessi was gone?

I opened my mouth but couldn't bring myself to say the words. I didn't want to think it. I was with her just last night! Granted, she wasn't there when I woke up, and her boxes were gone… A coldness flushed over me as I figured out I'd been wrong. I'd thought she just put the boxes away so she could do her job. Why would she have left without saying anything?

My eyes drifted to my phone. I picked it up, noting absently that there was a slight shake of my hands as I did so. I unlocked the screen, and her number was still there. I dialed it this time and put the phone to my ear. Emily stayed quiet through my silence, though she did start pacing the room in front of me. The phone rang and rang… until it cut off.

She wasn't picking up.

"Did you speak to her?" I asked, looking up at Emily. "Did she tell you she was leaving?"

Emily scowled at me. "I had to hear she was leaving from another source. I called her, and she must have been on her way there in her car already. That was an hour ago.

I would have come here immediately, but I was at home and I wasn't properly dressed."

"What did she say?"

It didn't sit well with me that Jessi was closer to Emily that she would talk to her instead of me, but if there was a way to change things…

"She didn't say much," Emily admitted. "To be honest, I don't know a lot of what went down between the two of you. I just have a bunch of rumors, most of which she confirmed. She sounded fine over the phone but I know that she's not, and it's because of you. She ran because she thought you would put her through more heartbreak."

Jessi…

"Why didn't she just talk to me…?"

It hurt to think that she would rather run from me than talk to me. Just what did she think last night was? Or the other night? I hadn't exactly clarified anything myself, but surely she knew my words from yesterday were sincere? I might have tried to lie to myself after our first time together, to convince myself I felt nothing for her. I knew that wasn't true anymore. If she had just asked me yesterday…

I never did give her that apology, though. And I didn't say everything that I should have, just what I thought she needed to hear to get her to stay. I should have asked if she was going to stay instead of assuming she would just because I said so.

"Fuck," I muttered, dropping my face into my hands. I'd made a lot of mistakes with Jessi.

"I guess you finally realize that you were in the wrong,"

Emily said, though her voice was completely sarcastic. "Well, that's good, but what I want more than you realizing is you doing something. Whatever it is you've broken in my friend you will fix it, or else. I don't know or care what's happened between the two of you since you've been back here, but dammit, you will fix it!"

Her voice rose as she spoke until she was shouting at me, and I leaned back in my chair, feeling chastised. I was more than a little stunned at her vehemence, though there was still a small part of me not over the shock that Jessi was gone.

"I haven't done anything to hurt Jessi," I started, trying to defend myself. "She probably just got the wrong idea because we haven't talked about anything—"

I cut myself off at her laugh full of derision as she folded her arms and cocked her hips to one side. She arched an eyebrow at me as she smirked.

"Oh, big brother. Don't tell me that along with a black heart you happen to have a selective memory as well? I know I just said I didn't know or care what happened between the two of you, but I've heard rumors from reliable sources, and we both know you've been mean to her in the past."

That was more than enough to shut me up. I didn't have to think back to know what she meant. I'd put Jessi down plenty of times, and it wasn't like I'd cared if other people heard.

"On your first day at the hotel," Emily started, "I heard you picked a fight with her. You didn't think she could have got her job here fairly. And don't think I missed what happened when you came to the mansion. When you left me to go running after Dad and ran into her. I heard the words you said about her, making a snub about the help using the front door. Oh, and there's plenty more if we start digging into the past." She gave a snort and sneered at me, tilting her head back so she looked down her nose at me. "Wow, big brother. I knew you were a douche, but to that girl? You were an absolute bastard."

My fists clenched on my thighs where she couldn't see as she listed out all the callous words I'd thrown at Jessi. She was right, our past was even worse. Back then Jessi had been around me a lot more than she was now.

"You know nothing about what's been going on between me and Jessi," I said, sounding a little defensive even to my own ears. "And it's none of your business anyway; I don't give a damn what you have to say. Now, please get out."

She didn't. Little sis was done listening to me. Forever, it would seem.

"That woman," she said, pointing a finger at me. "Jessi? She loves you. She fucking loves you, Trent! She's always loved you. I didn't tell her this, but even before you left and I was a little kid, I would see how she would make eyes around you every time you walked into a room. And you have always, always, thrown it back in her face. I kept silent then because I didn't know how to talk to you before, but I am fed up. I'm not just going to keep watching it anymore."

I was stunned, once again. In my mind, I wondered just what my sister had seen all those years ago. I tried to find some sort of defense for myself, some protest. Could there really be anything to find? I couldn't blame my family issues on it because it was my choice to be an ass to Jessi.

Hell, if I was honest with myself, I was an ass to them all and something of a tyrant, or Emily suddenly treating me so harshly wouldn't be so shocking. Her temper had never been aimed at me, but that was more because she didn't know me, and partially feared me, than that she had nothing against me.

I had a lot of making up to do. And not just to Jessi.

The question now was even if I wanted to try, could I? I looked up at Emily, the sister that I never knew, that I always thought was nothing but a meek, spoiled child but was now showing me colors I hadn't seen before. Had my brothers ever felt the same way, that they didn't know how to talk to me? My father, who was always trying to get me to come home, and my stepmom who made attempts to get close to me I always rebuffed… what about her?

I hadn't treated them much like family at all, and here Emily was, telling me to get her friend back.

"You better go after her, Trent," she said, voice suddenly quiet like she'd blown off all her anger while she'd screamed at me. "I don't care about whatever else you do, and you're going to have to figure out how to do it, but please bring Jessi back home. Soon, if you don't mind."

Home… this was Jessi's home. And I'd been the one to run her off. I watched Emily turn and walk out of my office, closing the door behind her especially gently.

I should go after Jessi. Not just for my sister's sake, but for my own.

JESSI

My alarm clock went off, waking me up from a pleasant dream. As I looked up at my new ceiling, lying in my new bed, waking up to a new day, I had the sudden urge to cry. Because my dream of being back home, surrounded by my friends and family, had been great, so much better than I could have expected it to be.

"I want to go back home," I whined out loud to myself.

But no matter how badly I wanted it, I had no plans to head back to the hotel in Charlotte after I'd run away not that long ago.

I got out of bed and went and got ready for the day reluctantly. On the way to work I tried calling Emily, but my friend wasn't picking up.

"Are you mad at me for leaving?" I asked, scowling at my phone. "Just pick up, would you! I could use a friend right now."

By then, I'd made it to the hotel, and I had to put the

phone away so I wouldn't get into trouble. As soon as I walked in, I was taken to task.

"Hey, newbie!"

I started at the loud call and looked up at the reception. Two people stood there, a woman and a man. It was the woman who had called out to me.

"Yes?" I said timidly, shifting my feet, wanting nothing more than to turn and run off to work.

"You forgot the entrance again or what? And aren't you a bit late? What, were you on the phone with your boyfriend so long you forgot when you were supposed to get into work?"

I tilted my head a little to the side. "I'm… late? But…"

I was reaching for my phone to check, but she scoffed at me, giving me a scornful look Trent would have been proud of.

"Just get to your station in the kitchen, would you?" the guy said. "You know what happens when you show up late, don't you?"

It had happened to me a few times already in the past couple weeks since I'd been at the new hotel. I made a quick bow as my heart started to beat a little in panic, then I practically ran in the direction of the hotel's kitchen. I prayed the whole way that I was in the clear. But then I got there…

"Jessi!"

I was startled for the second time that morning, only this time, the person called out my name. He wasn't the head chef, but he was a guy that didn't particularly like how I intruded on his life either. In his head, he probably thought I'd come to ruin any possible chance of him getting a promotion with my good performance. In the beginning, he'd hoped I would fail, and when I didn't, he'd used every moment possible to give me shit just to try and put me down.

After years of putting up with it from Trent, not just anyone was going to affect me that badly. More than anything, he was annoying.

"Excuse me," I murmured, keeping my head ducked down so he wouldn't see the irritation in my eyes.

"Why are you late again?" he asked, voice sharp.

"I'm not late, sir," I said quietly.

"You are late if you get here and half of the staff is already in here!" he snapped back. "Look around and tell me if half the kitchen staff made it here ahead of you."

I looked around, and sure enough, it was true. I winced, knowing this wasn't helping my case. But I hadn't been late! I had my schedule memorized, and I knew it was still some minutes until my official shift time.

Not that I could say that out loud because I knew these guys would just flay me over it.

"I'm sorry, sir," I muttered.

He huffed. "You think an apology will make everything okay, huh? I don't know what you did at the main branch, but things here are a little different, Jessi. You need to get your act together before you get your ass handed to you. Hurry up and get to work already. You're late enough as it is."

I watched his back as he walked away, then moved slowly over to my station. It was smaller than the one I used at the hotel back in Charlotte, and I had to share it. My new colleagues didn't bother hiding their snickers and whispers as work went on, glad I'd gotten in trouble again. They were pretty tight-knit, a lot like the old guys I worked with. Of course they would give me a hard time, being the outsider. It was to be expected, but maybe not to the extent that I'd felt it already.

After working through the morning and stopping in midafternoon, I was feeling hungry and exhausted. I was a little fearful to go on my break without finishing my work for the day, so I stuck it out until I could leave for a breather.

The hotel itself was pretty beautiful, and just outside there was a nice view of the beach. I felt some longing, wanting to go down that way for a walk, but it was too risky while I was still on shift.

***

"I MADE A MISTAKE, EMILY," I muttered, sighing wistfully. "I just want to go home, but why won't you pick up my calls so I can tell you?"

It had been hard enough to push aside my pride so I could call her. I didn't want to admit I'd made a mistake, even though I felt that way every day. I mean, dealing with Trent might have been hell for me had I stayed, but anything would feel better than knowing that everyone was bullying me for their amusement.

Two weeks felt like a long fucking time. As beautiful as the place looked, as great as being by the beach was, I hated my time at the hotel more than anything and wanted to run back home into the comfort of my mom's arms.

The staff particularly acted as if I'd personally offended them by getting myself transferred here. I guess transfers were pretty rare to begin with, because finding employees with such high-level standards that the hotel would agree to transfer instead of just letting them go, wasn't exactly easy. As far as I knew, there had only ever been two other transfers at the hotel in Charlotte for the past decades it had been running.

"Bastards, all of them," I muttered. "They are such bastards, Emily. They're all so damn greedy, and they're mean to me because I managed to get a transfer. I'm such an easy target for them. What am I supposed to do?"

There was no Emily there to answer me, and after a few more minutes of taking in some fresh air, I decided to go back inside so I wouldn't get into more trouble.

Why did I ever think this was a good idea? I thought to myself.

If I wasn't at the hotel and taking shit from the rest of the staff, I was walking around and talking to myself because I couldn't get a hold of Emily. I spent my free time in my tiny apartment, which somehow managed to seem even smaller than the one I'd had in Charlotte.

I regretted my hasty decision to leave, and then picking this particular branch hotel to head out to. If my friend would just answer me when I called... I could tell her everything, and she would help me, and I would ask to be allowed to go back home. I knew I could have just gone to the manager to tell him I wanted to go back… but the manager here didn't like me either. I met him on the first day, and he'd looked down on me, probably thinking I knew someone high up at the other hotel which was why I managed a transfer.

Well, it was true, but I'd run away because of that person, and he sure as fuck didn't help me. They knew I was at least good at my work. I'd been put in the hot seat the first few days, they were probably hoping to see me fail, and instead, I got praise. They'd halved my workload and a part of me was grateful while the other was disgruntled. I was pretty sure if they'd thought I was terrible, they might have kept things as they were so that I could get into even more trouble.

If only I wasn't so good at my job.

Could I go back and face Trent?

That was the question that made me hesitate all throughout the first week of being there. I only started calling Emily in the second week because I'd been unsure of myself. I thought it would be easy to deal with Trent. What the fuck did I even run away for? I was mature, wasn't I? Adults were supposed to deal with their problems, not walk away from them.

Finally, the end of my shift came, and I left the hotel feeling relieved. I was walking back to my apartment when my phone rang. It was so unexpected it made me jump, but when I pulled it out and saw Emily's name on the screen, I was relieved.

Finally!

"Emily," I said quickly as soon as I'd answered the call. "Emily, I need to talk to you."

There was a sigh on the other end. "I need to talk to you, too."

Her voice sounded so subdued I lost my urgency, wondering what had happened.

"I have something I need to tell you," she said. "It's supposed to be a secret, but I want you to hear it. It's about my dad."

"Is he ill?" I asked hesitantly. "There hasn't been any news at all…"

"My father isn't sick," Emily blurted out. "He was never sick. He just wanted my brothers to come back home, so he made it up and had me help him. He's putting off seeing them because he knows they'll notice the moment they see him that there's nothing wrong with him, and he's worried they'll leave again."

That gave me pause. To say I was shocked would be an understatement. Matthew Thompson was never quite so manipulative. This plan was something I would expect to see Trent using before his father. Was the man that desperate to have his children back? I knew for Trent to come back home, he had to have been worried about his dad. How would he react when he found out?

"That's the kind of family that I have, Jessi," Emily said, her voice sad. "So do you want to tell me why you were calling me over and over now?"

"No," I murmured. "I'll call you back, Emily."

I cut the call because I had some more thinking to do. I'd been so ready to go back, but now I wasn't so sure.

Was that really what I wanted to go back to? Did I want to have anything more to do with that family? Having heard what Emily wanted to tell me, I felt more like I'd dodged a bullet. The Thompsons had always seemed like the perfect family on the outside. I knew some of their secrets that made that image not entirely true. But this was even worse.

Behind all that wealth the family held, the glass smiles they gave to people in public, there were so many lies. So many hidden secrets and emotions they never let the world see. So much deceit. Trent was the perfect example of it all, and I had been in love with him for years.

Maybe… I was lucky, to be able to leave? Because in a way, I had escaped getting entangled with them. My heart felt heavy as I watched the sunset on the beach as I wondered, feeling conflicted.

Was it the right decision to leave home, in spite of everything?

21

TRENT

"Here are the documents you needed, sir."

I waved my hand at the secretary to leave them on the desk in front of me without looking away from the computer monitor, though I did spare her a glance when I heard the folder hit the desktop.

"Thank you," I murmured distractedly, pulling the keyboard closer to me to type something out.

"Any time, sir," she said, then walked out. I heard the door closing behind her.

I finished what I was working on, then pushed the keyboard to the side and reached for the new folder.

"Shit is getting a little too busy around here," I muttered to myself as I opened it up to look at the contents.

In the time since Jessi had left, I had been busy. So super fucking busy that I barely had the time for regrets, and still, I kept thinking about Jessi and how we'd left things, how my sister had all but commanded I go after her. I'd made the decision that I had to… but because I was an idiot, work came first.

If I was being honest with myself, I would admit to being afraid. So damn afraid about everything. The moment Emily had left my office, I'd been about to drop everything to run out and do what she'd wanted, to go looking for Jessi to bring her back. I only stopped myself at the last minute because I realized that wasn't like me at all.

Just what was happening to me?

It was terrifying for me because I'd always been in control of myself, ever since I was a teenager. I'd forced that control on myself, thinking it was the only way I could live. And then, out of nowhere, I needed someone else. It was a weakness that came out of nowhere for me, because I'd pretty much killed the word "need" in my vocabulary. If you needed, then you were opening yourself up to pain and disappointment.

And yet, I had this deep need for someone's presence, and that someone just had to be Jessi of all people. I'd never felt that way towards anybody, not since Mom died, anyway.

The terror that arose from it was something foreign, something I'd thought I got rid of a long time ago. I'd stopped being afraid of things by the time I was six, after Mom was gone, and Dad was too busy to even be there for me, all I'd had was myself. I'd taught myself to kill fear and had lived without it for two decades. So what the fuck was happening now?

A knock on the door made me look up. I was distracted anyway, I'd only got to the middle of the document before what I was reading blurred and I focused on my thoughts. The secretary walked in, and I arched an eyebrow her way.

"Can I help you with anything?"

"A few calls for the meeting came in, sir," she said. "I wanted to ask you for permission before setting any meetings."

I didn't want to take any meetings. All of this was supposed to be my dad's job, and the old man was still hiding himself away in the mansion. I'd gone over to try and speak to him a few times, only to be rebuffed, and it just left me more confused about the whole situation. It had been nearly a month since I'd come back home, and there was no news of his health, so I was still handling things that should have been his to handle.

The meetings were particularly annoying because the people that came in were more about sucking up to me or talking down to me because I was there in place of my dad. It was so damn annoying I'd stopped taking meetings last week. I was busy enough as it was without them.

"Are they important?" I asked because that was all I cared about.

"I'm afraid they are, sir," she said, almost apologetically. "I could set them up for some time next week?"

I nodded with a bit of relief. "I think that would be for the best."

"I'll get on it."

She walked back out, and I leaned back into my seat with a heavy sigh.

I needed to talk to Dad before then. I wasn't sitting in one more fucking meeting!

It wasn't like I got anything from them, anyway. When I did pay attention, resolutions weren't met, and follow up meetings had to be set. It was a far cry from the success I'd had with my own business, and it was so damn frustrating. I'd thought I was on my way to a beautiful career, but clearly, I still had much to learn about the business world. It was still annoying to learn I wasn't as unflappable as I'd thought.

"Why did I have to be a Thompson?" I asked my empty office.

I got no answer, as expected, but that only made me even more irritated.

I hated the family name. I hadn't given much thought to it when I was younger, and I only started to know its true weight when I got to high school. When I'd walk to school, and I would have people fawn over me because of the name and the family it was attached to. I'd even toyed with getting my name legally changed, perhaps to my mom's maiden name, but I knew Dad would never stand for it.

More than anything, I hated what it all stood for. People saw my name as something to be proud of, but I would rather hide it because all it reminded me of was a man who was fooled into a marriage when he still should have been grieving, and a woman who deluded a man because of her greed and needs.

I ran my hands over my face, feeling done with it all.

"Why can't I go back home?" I wondered out loud. "I miss the mountains. It's so much easier to hide from it all there. Hide from them."

I couldn't just up and leave, though. No matter how

much resentment I held for my father, he was still my family, and I had my obligations. I had no intention of dropping them and leaving because I wanted to hide. It would be too shameful; my pride would never be okay with it.

There was another knock on the door, and I looked at it curiously with a small frown. If it was the secretary coming back to ask authorization for more meetings, I was going to refuse this time.

"Come in," I called.

The door opened, and I was shocked to see Emily come in.

"What are you doing here?" I blurted, but really, I was just surprised she was polite this time, even taking the time to knock. It was a far cry from her behavior when she was last here.

"I came to see you," she said matter-of-factly.

She was dressed more or less the same as the last time I saw her, in a designer dress and a pair of heels, with painted nails and her hair styled to fall around her shoulder, down her back. Only the colors were darker than last time, and I didn't know if that was a clue to her mood or not.

"What did you come to see me about?" I asked cautiously.

She sighed as she slumped into the chair across my desk and looked up to meet my eyes with a determined gaze.

"It's about Dad," she said.

Immediately, I perked up. "What, did something happen?"

She waved a hand at me. "Don't get so alarmed; Dad is fine. In fact, he's always been fine. There was never a heart attack. Maybe a little heartbreak but that's it."

"I'm sorry?"

"How many ways can I say this, big brother?" she said with a heavy sigh, jumping out of the chair to pace the room, arms crossing over her chest. It was just like last time, only I figured this time around she had a different reason for not wanting to look at my face. "Dad deceived all of you, and he made me keep his secret. He wanted you guys to come back home, and he wanted you to help expand the business. He hasn't been ill at home at all. Honestly, it's like he's on vacation or something."

What the fuck?

I narrowed my eyes at her, not wanting to believe it. I liked to think I knew my little sister a bit more than I did before, and I didn't think she would lie about something like this. It was just so hard to believe my dad would come up with such a devious plan, all for what? To have me and my brothers back home, working hard for him, as it should be?

Seriously, Dad?

"Is everything you just said true?" I asked.

Emily met my gaze and nodded, tilting her chin up slightly at my hard look, clearly refusing to be cowed. "Yes," she said simply.

Fuck.

I didn't ask anything more, taking her word for it. I

stood up, picked up my coat, and left the room. Emily called out to me, but I ignored her. I stopped at the secretary's desk.

"I'll be leaving now," I said, ignoring her shocked reaction. "My father will be back in the office soon. Let him know the progress."

"Sir?"

I kept on walking. If Dad didn't show up for his job, then that was his problem. I'd wasted enough time around here. Dad hadn't bothered to see any of us, me, Mason, or Kevin, and all because he was pretending to be ill? I was already on the verge of breaking, and Emily's confession was the last straw for me.

I went back to my room at the hotel and cleared it out. I had some stuff at the mansion, but it wasn't anything I couldn't live without. I'd let myself get fooled because of my concern for my father, and I wanted to go off and lick my wounds and pretend none of this ever happened, back to my mountains. I hadn't eaten, but I didn't even pause as I packed my stuff up, went down to my car, jumped in and drove for home.

The perfect escape, I thought to myself. The perfect little reason to run away from everything.

Maybe it was unfair, but I couldn't help but think of Jessi's disappearance in light of my dad's betrayal. I'd wanted to see her, to find her as Emily said, but right then, I killed that idea.

Jessi leaving me had hurt badly enough. It had hurt a lot deeper than I was willing to admit. It had been so easy for her to leave, that I wondered what she thought of me. I'd never given her reason to think anything positive of me, so that was my fault.

But the short time we'd had together had been so sweet. While I was with her, I had felt so different from how I was every day for the past decade. I'd harbored some hope, I'd hoped to help Dad out and that she and I could work something out.

Jessi threw that away, not me. I realized the thing holding me back, besides the fear, was the hurt. If I went after her, wouldn't she just throw me away again? Just like my father, who was now resulting to tricks to try and get me to return to the fold when all he had to do was fucking talk to me like I was his son, not his heir.

I'd anticipated getting back home so much, but my arrival was completely anticlimactic. Once I got back, I went inside, leaving my suitcase in the car, and headed straight for my bedroom. I had a balcony with a perfect view of the mountains, and I breathed a sigh as I stood there, looking out.

I watched the sunset from the mountains, feeling lost for the second time in my life, the first time having been after my mom's death.

What the fuck was I supposed to do now?

22

TRENT

I was back home, but I wasn't in the mood for work. So I stuck around at home, lazing around.

It was something new to me. I'd worked hard because I knew it was the way out for me. I'd rarely taken days off, and when I did, it was to go out hiking. Never to stay at home and do nothing, it wasn't in my fucking genes. Work, work, work that was all us men ever did in our family. Maybe that was the fucking problem, the reason that we were so dysfunctional as a family.

On my third day back, I woke up and checked my phone. It was mid-morning, and the nit-picky side of my personality was scandalized. Usually, I was up at the break of dawn. I normally went for a run around the neighborhood before heading back in for a shower, then got dressed and ready for work.

Instead, I got out of bed in an old pair of sweats and a t-shirt, scratching my head as I yawned. I'd stayed up late contemplating some useless shit I couldn't even remember, but at least it kept my mind off my problems for the time being.

I wasn't going anywhere, but I headed for the shower anyway. One thing I was refusing to fudge on was showering when I woke up. I brushed my teeth as the shower warmed up, and as I blinked the sleep from my eyes, I caught a glance at my reflection.

Well, damn, I thought. I looked like shit.

I hadn't shaved for the past few days, and I had a nice little beard growing in, a pale blond one that wouldn't be too noticeable to others but it was enough to get me to frown. I had bed hair too, and I ran my hands through it, feeling a few knots in the growing locks.

"I need a haircut," I decided. I'd have to get it before I went back in to work or people would stare and start more rumors.

I finished brushing my teeth and jumped into the shower. I took my time, letting the hot water pour over my skin, trying not to think of the two times I'd woken up after Jessi left me alone to wash away the evidence of what had happened between us. I couldn't help it though, and I thought back to those two nights as well.

"Fuck," I growled to myself, looking down at my rising cock.

I ended up getting myself off before I got out of the shower. I stood in front of my bathroom mirror to blow dry my hair and shave off the growing beard. Once I was satisfied with my look, I left the bathroom.

Back in the bedroom, I moved to the closet to try and

decide what to wear. Most of my wardrobe consisted of formal wear or hiking gear and my work out clothes.

Maybe I could go out today. My fridge was getting a bit empty. Besides, I was going to have to get back into the outside world at some point, might as well start small.

I picked a shirt, a pair of slacks, and a belt, then put them on. I thought about putting on socks, but decided against them, picking out a pair of loafers. Dressed, I went to my living room and turned the TV on for background noise, picking up the tablet I'd left on my coffee table to check out the news.

An hour later, my doorbell rang.

I frowned to myself because I almost never got visitors. The few people who did visit me at home were family. Usually, it was just Mason. Kevin didn't visit me, and Dad only dropped by at the office. I wasn't sure who it was, but I got up to check my security monitor.

"Really?" I muttered, scowling at the man on the monitor.

I was suddenly glad I'd decided not to dress and walk around my home like a slob for the day. Dad had come for a visit.

With reluctance, I went to open the door. Dad had his back to me as he looked up and down the street, turning when he realized I was right behind him.

He looked just as I'd last seen him. We both had the same physique and were at the same height. He had the same blond hair and grey eyes as me. Plenty of people commented on how much we looked like each other, way too many in fact, like Dad was exactly what I would look like in twenty or so years. He was dressed in a polo-shirt and slacks with loafers, not so different from how I was dressed. My eyebrows shot up because it was rare to see Dad out of a suit, but I was more surprised to see him at my doorstep at all.

"Nice place you have here," he said, looking around again before meeting my gaze. "Are you going to let me in, or are we going to do this at the door?"

I was so tempted to just have it out with him right there, but I didn't need my neighbors looking on at any spectacle. Dad would be leaving soon but I still had to live here. No need to make things harder for myself. Still, it was with reluctance that I stepped aside for him to walk in.

"What are you doing here, Dad?" I asked, instead of a real greeting, just like he'd done. "Don't you have a hotel to look after?"

He turned to give me a wry smile. He walked to the other side of my living room, where the glass gave the perfect view outside. Not as good as from my balcony, because there I could at least breathe in the mountain air along with the view, but I would hardly be taking Dad to my room.

"I wondered how long I should wait to see you," he said. "Before and after you found out the truth."

"You can say it bluntly," I said, voice thick with sarcasm. "You mean after I found out that you used Emily to lie about you having a heart attack, just to get me home."

He had his back to me, hands in his pockets so I couldn't figure out what he was thinking, and exactly what he'd come to me for. After a minute of silence, I let out an explosive sigh.

"Seriously, Dad. What did you come here for? If its business, it can wait until I get back to my office. I'm taking the whole week off."

Dad let out a sigh. "I came here to talk. Like really talk, like I should have a long time ago."

I was left stunned, and I couldn't say anything to that. It was exactly what I'd wanted, but now that he was here, I wasn't sure I wanted to have this talk at all.

"We can start with your mother," he said, his voice going gruff. "I know I wasn't there for you as I should have been when she passed away. I was too busy dealing with my grief at the time, and by the time I realized that it was too late. You were still a young boy, but you were slowly making yourself independent."

I swallowed back the sudden lump in my throat. "You don't have to say anything, Dad."

He went on as if he hadn't heard me.

"When I realized what I'd done, I thought about how to fix it. I knew I couldn't be there for you as much as I would like, and I didn't want to leave you to be raised by nannies. So, I figured it was time to start looking for a second wife, maybe too soon, and I found her and brought her home. I wasn't sure I could love again after losing your mother, but I grew to love her, and I started a new family with her. Again, it was too late by the time I realized you were isolating yourself from that family instead of trying to be a part of it. That was my second mistake."

My hands fisted at my sides as he continued speaking.

It wasn't out of anger. My fingers were shaking, but even tightening them didn't stop the fine trembling that was overtaking my body.

"I wasn't sure what to do," he continued, "as I watched you grow up looking at your half-siblings and stepmother like strangers. I tried to bridge that gap so many times, only to be met with failure, making numerous mistakes I stopped counting."

"Why are you saying all this?" I cut in, speaking through gritted teeth, unable to stand much more. "Why are you saying all of this only now, huh?"

Finally, he turned around. His lips were flattened, and his eyes had a suspicious sheen to them.

"Because, Trent, I came here to apologize to the son I never did right by. I know this is coming late, but I would like to change that."

I sneered at him. "You're right about one thing—this is way too late. I'm not sure I even care anymore, so you just wasted a trip."

"Why can't you give them a chance?" he asked with a narrowing of his eyes.

"I have given them chances," I countered. "I talk to them, don't I? Besides Emily, but what am I supposed to talk to her about?"

"What about Alice?" he asked, voice neutral.

I let out a harsh laugh. "There's even less reason for me to talk to your wife. That woman is nothing but a menace, and you have no idea how many times I wish she never existed or come into our lives."

"Trent!"

"Do you even have any idea what her brother did to me?" I shouted back, and that gave him pause. It was obvious that he had no idea. "And you seriously call yourself my father?"

We stood on opposite sides of the room just watching each other for a while. My body still trembled, while Dad just stood there looking calm. I knew he was a little flustered because I'd had time to read him under his professional mask.

"What do you mean about Alice's brother?" he finally asked.

I let out a derisive snort. "Do you even care?"

"Trent," he said my name in warning.

I watched him in defiance for a moment before speaking.

"You know he worked at the boarding school you sent me too, right? Right up until middle school, and then I made you send me to a high school with no affiliations to that school, and I ended up in the same place as Jessi."

He nodded, prompting, "Go on."

"He was my warden at the school. That gave him the right to administer disciplinary action, only, he didn't always report it, just because he could."

Dad's eyes were narrowed, and I wondered if he was clued in already.

"He did something to you," he voiced it as a statement, not a question.

I gave him a grin for his trouble. "You guessed it, Dad. The man was a bastard. And do you know what that bastard used to tell me, when he would pick me up for no reason, lock me in a room with him, then belt me until I was begging him to stop, and he still did it? He kept telling me how you were all starting a new family, how I was going to get tossed aside. And of course his sister's little brats would be heir to everything, and she would hand him a nice little nest egg for his trouble in looking after an unwanted brat like me."

Dad was looking at me with a shocked look that was at the same time the most satisfying thing, and yet not. I hated reliving the memories, but I wanted him to know. To realize just how deep my resentment for him went, and how it wasn't all that unfounded.

"In all that time, Dad, you never helped me. And for years, I had to put up with that bastard's shit. Then I decided if you were all going to throw me away anyway, I might as well be the one to leave first."

"Son, I never would have—" he started, but I cut him off with a slash of my hand.

"Save it, Dad," I growled harshly. "I'm not looking for pity, or an apology, or any assurance. I just figured you might as well know, because you always wondered why I never wanted to go back home. Why I never wanted anything to do with that woman."

"Alice had nothing to do with this," he said.

I watched him for a moment, before breaking into chuckles. Suddenly feeling exhausted, I walked over to the couch and slumped into it while Dad remained standing. I couldn't even look at him anymore because I didn't want to see the expression on his face. I meant it when I said I didn't want an apology from him. It was way too fucking late for that.

"Trent," he said, his voice firm. "I'm going to look into this now that I know. I can also promise you one thing: Alice had no hand in what her brother was doing. She wouldn't have known, and she's never given him anything, so everything he told you was a lie. Ever since she heard about you she sincerely wanted to meet you, wanted to be a mother to you. I know she would never replace Mom for you, she doesn't for me either, but she wanted to try. The least you could have done was given her a chance."

I pressed my lips together, not wanting to admit he was right. That I could have been wrong about everything, and because of the misunderstanding, I'd missed out on far more than I should have. I'd missed out on the family I could have had if only I had opened up and spoken up sooner.

Back then, I had made a choice. And it wasn't the right one.

"I won't force you on this matter," Dad said after a moment of silence. "You're a smart boy, and I know you can think for yourself. And also, Jessi makes the finest tiramisu I ever tasted. I don't know what happened between the two of you, and I don't care, but if you don't bring her back to Charlotte, I will have your balls for it."

I couldn't help but let out a laugh because his words mirrored Emily's, but then I let out a sigh and looked over at Dad. He stood there a little awkwardly, not quite meeting my gaze. Then he walked over to me, patted me on the shoulder, and headed for the front door to let himself out.

"Well," I muttered. "I guess I wasn't any easier, was I?"

It would be so easy to put all the blame on my dad, but I knew that would be wrong. I was smart enough to know that part of the communication problem between us started with me. I never gave Dad much of a choice when it came to how to approach me. If I'd come clean, talked instead of waiting for him to make the first move, it would never have reached the point of him faking a heart attack to get me home.

I needed to make a change. It was way past time, and my thoughts had already been leading me in that direction for a while now.

To start with, just because he'd mentioned her, I figured I might as well bring Jessi back to the fold.

I ran to my bedroom where I'd left my phone on the nightstand and made a call for the family helicopter to pick me up.

23

JESSI

I was in the middle of work, distracted as always. It was as if I was here in body but not in spirit.

The kitchen at the Myrtle Beach hotel had different rules than from where I came from. I'd got so used to my old job that I tended to do things on automatic when I wasn't paying proper attention—which was rare in and of itself, because I took my job very seriously—but I was still stewing with myself over my decision as to whether to go back to Charlotte or stay in my current position.

I could stay...

But four days after I'd had the thought that I might not have made the best idea with the transfer, I realized I was still miserable. Even more so, because I'd come to know in the ensuing days that things could get worse. My new coworkers had upgraded from occasionally acting like assholes, to outright bullying, reminiscent of high school.

It was so fucking annoying. I'd get into work, go to my locker in the staff room, only to realize my uniform was missing. Then I had to track down a new one, sign on a bunch of forms, and when I finally got a new set, I went back to my locker only to find my old uniform there, dirty when I'd left it clean. While I wasn't in uniform, I wouldn't be allowed to work in the kitchens, so it was like I was slacking off at work.

There were other little things, like them snubbing me when a bunch of us were in the staffroom for meal breaks or tripping me up when I got near them. Thankfully, no one had tried it while we were in the kitchen, or I might have tripped into one of the many hot cooking stations and burned myself or been otherwise injured. They were immature, but they weren't taking it too far.

But I'd gone through high school, and I knew if it didn't stop soon, then at some point, someone might try it. There had been some sabotage here and there as well with people messing with my recipes, and I'd have to start all over instead of allowing anything less than my best be served up to the guests.

Honestly, the behavior was getting old quickly, but I was giving it a little time before I made a formal complaint, since I doubted arguing back would be of much help. Whether the manager would take action or not... well. That, I had no idea about, but I had to hope.

Although, there was another option.

I could always go back...

But there were pitfalls with that plan as well, ones that I wanted to avoid. Running into Trent being one of them.

Not that it was my biggest problem. If I wanted to go back to the hotel in Charlotte, I would have to apply for another transfer, and again, I would have to go to the manager to get that done. His attitude towards me meant he wouldn't make it easy for me. He might outright refuse or he could delay it. Or pretend to agree to it at first, only for me to find out later that he was just pranking me.

Maybe that kind of thinking was a little overboard. I was turning this guy into a typical villain when he might not be that bad a guy. But that didn't necessarily mean he would be on my side either. Because, whether or not I had good reasons, the transferring back and forth was an inconvenience for both sides because of the paperwork involved. And the last thing I wanted was to make a nuisance of myself, so that was another reason why I was hesitating.

With so much to think about, I was distracted and not noticing what I was doing. I'd worked that way a few times, so at first, it wasn't a problem. Until I knocked into another worker there, who yelped and dropped the bowl they were holding. It was made of metal, and it dropped to the floor with a loud clang that caught everyone's attention and made everything come to a halt.

I would have been fine had I been back home because I was so used to the kitchen there. Here, it was a bit smaller, more cramped, and organized in a way that seemed disorganized to me.

If I had been back in Charlotte, there would have been a moment of silence, then good-natured laughter and ribbing from everyone else, teasing me about what—or who—I was daydreaming over.

Here, though…

"Jessi!"

I winced at the loud yell of my name, even as expected as it was. Slowly, I turned to look at the chef who'd called me. It was the same chef who'd been giving me a hard time since I got here, I'd never actually met the head chef here, and I was starting to wonder if the man was just lazy, or if this guy was him.

"Yes, sir?" I said meekly, clasping my hands in front of me and keeping my head ducked down.

Before, he'd looked for whatever excuse to give me shit, and I couldn't even blame him this time because it was my fault.

"What do you think you're doing?" he asked, his voice especially loud in the silence.

I fidgeted, shifting from foot to foot as I twisted my fingers together, my stomach tying itself up in knots. It felt like my lips were glued together, and it took a moment to part them, only words escaped me.

"Um… I…"

"You were daydreaming in the middle of work," he accused.

I couldn't say no, so I just kept silent. I wanted a hole to open up in the ground and swallow me whole. I didn't bother to check, but I knew the others were trying to hold in their snickers at my misfortune. I hadn't failed to notice how no one else got into as much trouble as I did.

"We're here to work, Jessi," he went on. "I don't know what it is that you were doing at the main branch, but we're serious people here. I don't know if you wanted to come down here or if you were sent away, but either way, you can't come here and bring the rest of us down just because you can."

I wanted to scoff when he said the 'serious people' part. But what followed had me holding back. I had neither wanted to come or was sent away, but I couldn't even open my mouth to defend myself. A fine trembling started in my body, and I blinked as my eyes started to sting.

"Everyone else, continue working. Jessi, move over here."

I sighed as I left what I'd been doing and went over to where the chef moved, out of the way of everyone else as they went on with their work. They didn't even bother to hide that they were listening in on our conversation, and I did my best to ignore them.

Why the fuck am I letting them get to me?

I knew better than to show weakness because that was when they went in for the attack. So when I looked up, my expression was stoic, and I pushed back my emotions. I thought back to school, on the few occasions I was sent to the principal's office and dealt with this as I did with that. I distanced myself from it emotionally, looking on dispassionately as the chef continued berating me. The others were outright making fun of me now, but I ignored that too.

Stay calm, I thought to myself. This is nothing like high school. The worst they can do is fire you, and it's not like finding jobs in other places would be hard with such a good record.

Not that I wanted to get fired but starting over might not be such a bad thing. I wouldn't have to stay at Myrtle

Beach, and I could find someplace close enough to Charlotte that I wouldn't be too far from my parents. The Thompson hotel was the biggest contender in the area, but there were a few other hotels I could try for.

"What is going on in here?"

The sudden interruption had everyone freezing again. My eyes blew wide as I registered the familiar voice, thinking I had to be mistaken. But I looked around, and sure enough, there he was. Dressed in a shirt, slacks, and loafers instead of the usual suit, with his hair falling over his forehead, but it was undoubtedly him.

"Who are you?" the chef asked, incensed at being interrupted. "And what are you doing in my kitchen?"

"Trent," he said bluntly, walking further into the room. His eyes traveled from me to the chef in curiosity. "And who are you?"

The guy looked offended that Trent had to ask, and puffed out his chest, fisting his hands on his hips.

"I'm the head chef around here," he said proudly.

I almost laughed, wondering if he meant that it was his given position or the position he imagined himself in because I believed the latter. Though I was worried, Trent's presence had made me feel lighter. He probably wasn't here today to make things even harder for me.

"Not anymore," he said, sounding almost cheerful as he put his hands in his pockets and faced the chef. "From now on, you no longer work here. Have your bags packed and yourself moved out of the premises. If you're still here by tomorrow, I will know. You'll receive your severance package. Good day, sir."

The chef was stunned, standing there gaping in shock, before he started stuttering.

"Who are you to come here and fire..." he started to argue, losing steam as his eyes widened. He gulped. "Trent Thompson?" he asked, suddenly looking small and fearful of the answer.

Trent gave his best smirk. "The one and only. And I'm afraid I'm going to have to steal the pastry chef. She is still very much needed at the main branch. If you would all excuse me."

He looked down expectantly at me. It took me a minute to realize what he wanted, and I started to walk out of the kitchen, him falling into step beside me. Once we were out, and hopefully away from earshot, I stopped. Trent turned to me again with that expectant look, only for it to dissolve into shock when I suddenly burst into laughter, that may have been part giddy and part hysterical.

"Thank you for that," I said, once I'd calmed down a little, wiping the tears from my eyes. "I don't know why I laughed so hard, but that was a nice sight to see."

Trent chuckled beside me. "Anytime," he teased, nudging my shoulder with his. Though his expression turned serious when I looked up to meet his gaze. "I wanted to talk to you. Do you mind following me back to my suite? I have one booked."

I didn't refuse, and he led us to an elevator, where we got on and went up several floors. We went to his room, and the first cursory glance told me it was beautiful. But I could hardly focus on it when Trent walked in behind me. He looked as handsome as I remembered, even more so perhaps, and I realized I'd missed him over the past few weeks.

"What did you want to talk about?" I asked, curious. And how was it I had dreaded this, but Trent was standing right in front of me, and all I could feel was a relief?

He took a deep breath, wiping his hands on his thighs. He paced slow steps to close the distance between us, and all I could do was watch him as my heart started to beat a little fast.

"I wanted to say I'm sorry."

I blinked, not comprehending the phrase. "I'm sorry, what?"

Suddenly, words were spilling out of his mouth. "I came because I realized I never apologized to you. And it was completely unfair of me to think you would stay when I hadn't even done that. I'm sorry for everything I've ever done to you, including our past together, and I'm also sorry that it took me this long to get my act together and find you. I meant it when I asked you to stay. So please, come back with me, Jessi."

I didn't know how to react. A part of me wanted to rail at him because I'd spent so much time feeling worried, and here he was, telling me everything I wanted to hear. My eyes stung again, and I blinked back the tears.

"Trent," I said his name in a whisper, and it was all I could get past the lump in my throat.

Like he understood what I was trying to say, Trent closed the space between us. His hands cupped my cheeks as I tilted my head and ducked down so his lips covered mine. I melted into the kiss, sighing at the familiar feel and taste of him, even after the weeks apart.

His mouth was rough against mine, and all I could do was clutch at him as he walked me backward, never once breaking from the kiss. I jumped a little when my back hit something hard and cold, probably the glass wall from the smooth feel of it through my clothes. I didn't even care that people might be able to see us from outside.

Trent had come for me, and it was more than I could have dared to hope for.

24

TRENT

 pulled away from the kiss to look down at Jessi, both of us panting.

I'd picked this room specifically because this was a sight I wanted to see. The room was sparsely furnished, with couches in one area and a bed further in. And even better, one wall was made entirely of glass, and it faced the beach. It reminded me of my home, save for the different view beyond the glass, and I planned to take Jessi home so I could have her against my glass wall there too. For the moment, this would have to do.

And damn the view was something fucking beautiful.

I took a moment to appreciate the view as Jessi leaned her head back against the glass. The beach was a nice backdrop, and light from the sun was right behind her, outlining her body. I pursed my lips as my eyes dropped down to her clothes. Things would be perfect if only we were both naked.

Patience, Trent, I chided myself.

"We should come back here again," I murmured, pushing a lock of dark brown hair behind her ear, then stroking my fingers along her neck, smiling when she shivered from the slight touch. "Would you like to?"

She arched an eyebrow. "If it's as guests, then sure. I didn't go on a lot of beach trips growing up."

Jessi blinked her bright, hazel eyes at me, and my breath caught in my throat. I wanted to ravish her against the glass wall, but I forced myself to have some patience. I wanted to convince her that being with me would be the best thing for her. I didn't want her trying to run from me again.

Tentatively, I leaned down for another kiss. I started softly this time, a chaste press of lips, moving my mouth gently against hers. Her arms around my neck held me close as I added a little pressure to the kiss, then nipped her bottom lip, alternating with little licks.

Jessi got a bit impatient herself, her fingers digging into the back of my neck as she held me close and parted her mouth. I took the invitation readily, letting my tongue slide between her lips and teeth to explore the inside of her mouth. Her body shuddered as she let out a soft whimper, rising up on her tiptoes to press her body against mine. I noticed because the ache starting in my neck eased up for a bit, but I hardly cared right then.

"Don't tease me," she whispered in between kisses. "I've waited for this for so long, Trent. Please?"

I let out a low moan at the 'please.' Usually, when women wanted things from me, they demanded them. When they asked to please have it, it was either a formality, or they were silently mocking me. I'd come to hate hearing the word 'please,' especially when it came from women. Hearing it from Jessi felt pretty satisfying.

"I'm not making either of us wait," I murmured as I pressed kisses all over her neck. "I'm just having a little fun first."

My lips landed on the spot just behind her ear, and she hunched her shoulders and let out a soft giggle. I paused then did it again, and she laughed.

"That tickles!"

I grinned against her skin, placed the last kiss on her cheek, and then pulled back. I looked down at her chef's uniform that I only realized she was still wearing.

"Do you mind if I take this off you?" I asked.

She nodded, pouting a little. "It's not a sexy outfit, is it?"

I shook my head, meeting her eyes for a second before my gaze dropped to the buttons I was slowly undoing.

"You look sexy in just about anything because you're you," I countered.

I finished unbuttoning the jacket and pulled her away from the glass so I could slip it off her shoulders, tossing it to the side. She had a top underneath, and I was tempted to pull that off as well, but instead just rested my hands on her waist.

Slow down…

All I could think in the time we were separated was how desperately I wanted Jessi. How, when I saw her, I would strip her down and fuck her against the nearest flat surface because I'd missed her so badly. That plan had changed.

"Let's move over to the bed?" I said, voicing it as a question because I felt just a little unsure. But this was Jessi, and I knew I didn't have to hide behind any walls with her.

She smiled up at me, took one of my hands, and tugged me over to the bed. It was placed in the corner of the room, where the glass wall ended to offer some privacy, even though we were several floors up.

I toed off my loafers as Jessi took off her shoes. My eyes landed on her ass as she crawled onto the bed, hips swaying. Once she was a bit higher and in the middle of the large king-sized bed, she rolled over onto her back, then sent a grin my way. I crawled after her, moving slowly until I was above her on all fours.

"You should probably be packing," I said in a whisper. "We're supposed to leave soon."

She grinned. "I never unpacked my things. It's all still in boxes in my room."

I arched an eyebrow down at her in surprise. "It's been weeks, though. What do you mean you haven't unpacked?"

She shrugged. "I've only been taking out what I need and putting back what I don't. Partly because I'm lazy. But mostly because I'd known I wouldn't be staying long. At first, I just missed home, but then I started to hate it here."

I scowled, remembering the guy I found yelling at her.

"Do I need to bring anybody forward for disciplinary action?"

Jessi snorted, lifting her hands to pat on my chest. "We're not in high school, Trent. You could probably make it happen, but it's fine. And you didn't wait for me to give you a proper answer. But in case you were wondering, I will be going back with you."

My heart thumped wildly as I smiled happily at Jessi. I could feel growing excitement of a different kind. But I hadn't suddenly forgotten the position we were in.

Jessi didn't wait for me to make a move, leaning up on one elbow, her other arm going around my neck as she tugged me down, then kissed me. I hummed as I kissed her back, kneeing her thighs apart and settling my body over hers carefully, until she was lying on her back with me on top of her, my upper body braced on my forearms, so I wouldn't crush her.

After several minutes of making out like a couple of teenagers, I pulled away from her mouth. Instead, my lips trailed over to her neck. My hands were back at her waist, and I slowly pushed her top up to slide a hand over her skin. She let out a shuddering sigh, and I left a nip on her neck.

"Trent," Jessi whispered, her voice ragged. "Please."

At her pleading with me again, I bit down on her neck. She yelped at the unexpectedness of it, and I smoothed it over with a lick. I stopped kissing her, pushing her top higher, until she lifted her upper body just enough to take it off and toss it to the side.

I placed both hands on her waist and slowly slid them up, my eyes staring right at her breasts. Her bra was in the way, but that wouldn't be the case for long. I cupped both breasts in my palms, squeezing a little, and Jessi gasped as her back arched, hips swiveling. I slid one of my hands underneath her, feeling for the clasp of her bra and undoing it.

Her hands stopped me just before I could take off her bra.

"You should strip down, too," she muttered petulantly, crossing her arms over her chest. "At least take your shirt off."

"As you wish," I said with a grin, shifting so I was kneeling on the bed.

She watched me as I undid the buttons of my shirt, her eyes following every bit of exposed flesh, my own eyes following the movement of her tongue as she licked her bottom lip. When I started undoing my belt, Jessi remembered herself, and she undid her pants. We stripped down, going slowly, our eyes following each other until we were both naked.

Then Jessi lay back down, legs spread, knees slightly raised, her arms reaching out to me. I could see a trace of vulnerability because of the position she'd put herself in, and I held her gaze as I returned to my previous position, bracing my body above hers.

"Fuck," I hissed, my eyes closing tightly for a moment as I felt her warm skin pressed against mine.

"Yeah," she breathed out, squirming under me. "This feels way too good, Trent."

"It's about to get better," I reassured.

I ducked my head down to kiss the top of her chest, moving down toward her breasts. I kissed and nipped my way to one nipple, flicking the pink bud with my tongue before sucking lightly on it. Jessi panted for breath as she dug her nails into my back, and I moved to her other nipple, giving it the same treatment.

Finally, feeling I'd tortured the both of us more than enough, I wrapped an arm around her waist to lift her hips. Taking the cue, she wrapped her legs around my waist, and we both let out a groan as the head of my cock rubbed against her sex. I rocked my hips gently, looking for her entrance until I felt her soft flesh give. I slid in slowly, holding my breath, hoping to gain some control. I could feel a bead of sweat travel down my spine, and I gritted my teeth until I was into the hilt.

After a moment of the both of us just staying still and breathing, Jessi tightened her legs around me and dug her nails even harder into my back. The move had her walls squeezing around my cock, and I released another groan.

"Move, Trent," she breathed, moving against me, even as I pressed her down into the mattress. "Please, move?"

Again, with that word. Like I couldn't help myself when I heard it, I did what she wanted, moving my hips. I started with slow, careful thrusts, adding a slight roll to my hips as I slid into her wet heat. I nipped my way up her neck until I covered her lips with mine. She opened readily for me, and my tongue slid into her mouth, tangling with hers. I picked up the pace just a bit, enjoying the breathy little noises she made with every one of my thrusts. When we needed a break to breathe, I'd break away from her lips to kiss all over her neck and the top of her chest, before slanting my mouth right back over hers.

This feels amazing, I thought. Wonderful was another word for it, like nothing I'd ever felt before. And I knew why; because for the first time, I wasn't just fucking. I was making love to Jessi, the only woman I would want to have that kind of experience with.

Jessi whimpered as her body began to shiver at me, and I could feel her walls convulsing around my cock. Groaning, I moved a little faster, a little harder, rewarded with a slight hitch in her breath. Jessi orgasmed, her head tilting back as she cried out her pleasure. I hit climax right behind her, and we clutched each other as our bodies shuddered.

We slumped to the bed, feeling sated, and I rolled us over so we were lying on our sides and I was holding her close. I buried my face in her hair, closed my eyes, and breathed in her scent.

"I'm taking you home, Jessi," I told her after a while.

She hummed. "Just don't forget my car and my things."

I released a sigh I hadn't realized I was holding.

Jessi's coming home with me, I thought to myself with a grin.

25

JESSI

We were in my car, driving back up to Charlotte with my stuff packed in the trunk and the back seat. Trent had insisted on driving, even though he'd looked at my car in disapproval at first, and I was in the passenger seat.

"If you came with the helicopter, why couldn't we just go back with it?" I asked. I wasn't complaining, just feeling curious and a little cramped in the car, especially when I didn't have driving as a distraction from boredom.

Trent shot a glance at me. "Well, I didn't want you to leave your stuff just so you would have to go back for it later, and it wouldn't all fit in the helicopter. Don't worry, though. I promise I'm a good driver."

"I'm not worried about that. If I didn't trust you, I wouldn't have given you the keys to my car to begin with."

He scoffed. "What, are you afraid I might harm your old scrap heap?"

The tone of his voice was teasing, so I knew not to take

him too seriously, even though the words sounded a bit familiar.

"Don't call my car an old scrap heap," I threatened. "It's all I've had for years. I got it pretty cheap, and I was ecstatic to get it."

"I'm sure you could afford a better one by now."

That gave me pause, and after a moment of thinking, I shrugged. I had enough cash in my bank account that I could probably buy myself another, nicer car. I could even afford a new car, probably, but that would just be a waste of resources to me. I was saving up. I didn't know what for, but I was going to let it sit pretty in the bank until I had a reason not to anymore.

"It must be uncomfortable for you," I said with a sigh. "My car is pretty small, and your height…"

"A bit," he admitted. "But it's not anything I can't handle for a few hours."

When we finally made it back to Charlotte, I was mildly surprised that Trent took us to the hotel and not the mansion. I pouted a little because I wanted to see my parents, but it wasn't a shock that he was still avoiding home.

"Let's go in," he said, shooting me a grin and jumping out of the car before I could follow.

I stared at him because this was the front entrance. What, did he expect me to carry my boxes up through the same entrance guests went through? It would make way too many people a little too curious about my life!

Before I could get my bearings, he was already around

the car and opening my door for me. I undid my seatbelt and stepped out, taking the keys from him.

"Just lock it for now," he instructed. "We can get everything later, I promise."

I sighed and did as he asked. "As long as you help me get them all up."

He grinned. "Definitely."

Trent took my hand, twining our fingers together, and practically dragged me behind him with his hurried steps into the hotel. I could feel my eyes widen because we were in full view of staff and guests as we hurried through the lobby to the elevators. He had a slight skip in his step the whole way, and I thought he even whistled.

We stepped into the elevator alone, though there were others standing there, probably waiting for one as well.

"Don't worry," he whispered to me as the doors closed. "It happens to me all the time."

I looked up to meet his eyes. "Really?"

He nodded. "When people recognize me, a lot of them tend to keep their distance. This is the first time I'm truly glad for it, though."

"Why is that?" I arched an eyebrow, but I was distracted by his openly happy expression, so much that it caught me off guard when he suddenly picked me up and whirled me around.

"Because you're finally back with me," he said in a sing-song voice. "I wanted to come after you so many times, you know? But I didn't, because I didn't know why. I've figured it out, though."

I met his eyes as my heart beat a little faster for a

different reason. "Why?" I asked, my voice coming out breathless.

He grinned, then ducked his head down close. I thought he was coming in for a kiss, and I closed my eyes. I felt his lips at my ear instead.

"I love you, Jessi," he whispered.

I gasped, and I could have sworn for a second my heart stopped. He pulled back to grin down at me, and I just stared at him, dumbfounded, taking the words in.

Trent just said he loved me...

Shit!

I opened my mouth to say something back. I didn't know exactly what, maybe to say I loved him too? But before I got the chance, the elevator doors opened, and Trent was dragging me back out. My eyes were fixated on his back as I replayed the words back in my mind.

He's different.

Trent wasn't acting quite like himself, and I wondered just how fast a person could change. He was no longer the same somber, somewhat mysterious man I'd met after a decade nearly a month ago. He was talking to me, he kept acting all playful like that sing-song thing in the elevator. He even told me he loved me!

"Is this a dream?"

I didn't realize I'd blurted the words out until Trent paused to glance over at me. We were already at the door to his suite, and he unlocked it and let us in.

"You're not dreaming," he said in reassurance. "But I guess you could say that I finally woke up. I wouldn't have gone looking for you otherwise because I'm a stubborn bastard."

I smiled wryly. "Well, I can't argue with that."

He shot me a betrayed look, and it made me laugh. But then I sighed, looking up at him with a frown.

"What exactly is going to happen to us?" I asked. "I ran away before because I didn't think we'd have a future."

Trent's expression suddenly turned solemn as he led me over to the couch and sat me down.

"We are going to have a future, Jessi. If you don't have any more plans that would take you away from me, I would very much love to spend the rest of my life with you."

His blunt nature sure hasn't changed, I thought, my jaw hanging open a little.

"I have no such plans," I squeaked out.

He was grinning again. "Good. The only real obstacle is my dad, but it's more what I'm going to do about him, than him being against a relationship between us."

"You finally got to see him?"

He nodded. "Yeah, though it's more that he came over to see me. I need to talk to him." He let out a heavy sigh. "I'd like to go back to my mountains, up in Asheville where my real home is. I don't want to let my dad down any more than I already have, either. For the first time, he asked me instead of just demanding I do shit."

"And that's a big deal?" I said slowly.

"Yeah, it is," he said. Then he gave me a pleading expression. "I'd hate to do this, and I'm sorry, but I'm going to leave you here for a little bit, okay? I'm trying to rebuild all my relationships so they aren't quite as messed up as before. Your friends will be coming to stay with you for the time being."

Before I could speak, to ask a question or protest, he pressed a quick kiss to my lips then he was rushing out of the room as I gaped at his back.

What the hell just happened? We weren't even back twenty minutes!

But I knew that fixing the relationship between him and his father was important. And if he was going to fix all the relationships he'd got wrong in his life, it was going to take a lot of time, and some massive groveling where his sister was concerned.

I wasn't sure how long I sat there like that, but then the door was opening again, and in walked the last two people I expected; Emily and Laura.

"Jessi!" they both squealed as they rushed me, and I jumped up so they wouldn't squish me into the couch. I couldn't help breaking out into giggles as they attacked me with bear hugs.

"We missed you so much," Laura said.

"I was about to track my brother down and beat him to a pulp," Emily added with a pout. "Or just drag you back myself."

I chuckled, hugging them both back tightly before I fell back on the couch, and they moved to sit on either side of me.

"You look exhausted," Laura said sympathetically, running a hand through my hair.

"Because I just came from a six-hour drive with no

stops," I said with a roll of my eyes. And it was right after Trent and I had a little extra action as we washed up before checking out.

"You've changed," Emily said with a narrowing of her eyes, leaning back as if to try and get a better look at me.

"What do you mean?"

She grinned. "You look happy for once. You're also acting all confident or some shit. And I could almost swear you're glowing." Her eyes widened. "Are you pregnant? I mean, the two of you sure work fast, huh…"

I shook my head slowly, trying not to let out how much that bothered me. Thinking that the 'glowing' was probably because the great sex was enough to make me perk up and give sly looks that had the both of them bombarding me with questions.

The thought stuck with me though, and I couldn't help remembering those damn pills. I regretted taking them now, instead of talking to Trent about it first. At the time, I thought for sure I was making the right decision, but was it the best in the long run?

I waited up for Trent to come back long after the other two had already left, with promises to look for me later. He finally walked in, sending a small smile my way.

"Can I ask you something?"

"Sure," he said, shrugging, then moving to join me on the couch. "You can ask me whatever you want."

I took a deep breath and decided to just go for it. "Do you remember the first time we slept together? How we didn't use any condoms?"

"Yeah, why?" he asked casually, only for his eyes to blow

wide open a moment later as he caught the implication. "You—"

"Before you get the wrong idea," I cut in. "No. I… went out and bought some pills afterward. I thought you'd get mad, if…"

My words trailed off as my expression crumpled, and I tried to keep myself from crying. Trent just sighed, then pulled me to his chest.

"I don't blame you for taking the pill, Jessi. But you won't have to from now on. I should have thought of protection first, and I'm sorry that I didn't, but I'm not sorry that I didn't use any either. If you don't want to take the pill… then don't."

I curled up against his chest, feeling so much relief that it sapped all the remaining strength in my body. I closed my eyes against the tears that wanted to fall, thinking how grateful I was that Trent had decided to come for me himself.

It was more than enough to show just how truly he cared for me, and I was determined not to waste the chance I'd been given with the love of my life.

I'm going to be yours now, Trent. For the rest of my life.

26

TRENT

"Are you sure you don't mind it?" Jessi asked, her voice small and muffled as she curled up against my chest.

I pursed my lips, feeling a slight ache in my chest. I'd never thought much about having children of my own but knowing Jessi could have been pregnant was having a strange effect on me.

"You don't have to feel bad about it," I told her gently. "You did what you thought was best for you at that time. You're allowed to think of yourself, Jessi."

Besides, back then I was still in a lot of denial about how I felt towards Jessi. If she'd come up to me to ask what to do, I felt afraid I might have told her to do exactly what she did. And the scare might have been enough to stop me from looking for her anymore, and I would have missed out on so much because of my pride and stupidity.

"Besides," I added, "there's no way to know that

anything came from it. You might not have got pregnant anyway, you were just taking precautions."

She sighed and finally lifted her head to look up at me. "I'm not exactly young anymore, you know. I'll be hitting thirty soon, so it's a race against biology, and if we're going to have any kids, I'd like it to be before I'm so old I get tired trying to take care of them."

I grinned down at her. "You've thought of having children before? With me?"

That had her blushing and ducking her head back down, and I let out a chuckle as I held her close again.

"I have," she admitted after a minute, voice small. "Ever since I was a teenager. Probably long before that, but let's say since I was a teen because that's when I knew how babies are made and born."

I hummed. "How many did you wish we'd have?"

She didn't answer me, and I chuckled again.

"Anyway," she said, a little wildly. "I had my period while I was at the beach, so I know I'm not. But... we always have the future, right?"

The words were stated tentatively, and she'd pulled back to look at me again. I noticed some traces of guilt lingering in her eyes, her expression, and I pecked a small kiss on her forehead.

"There's always the future," I reiterated. "So don't worry so much about what happened in the past, okay? I'm happy that you took the initiative, that you were thinking of protecting yourself. Let it go and we'll have ourselves a nice, bright future to try again, all right?"

The smile she gave me was a little shaky at the corners, but it was genuine.

"Do you mean it?" she asked.

I gave a serious nod. "Definitely. If it's what you want, we can try. We could see a doctor, just to make sure nothing is wrong first. Although I would have loved to have you all to myself, at least for a little while," I added with a sigh.

"You can have me as much as you want, Trent," she reassured. "In fact, you can have me right now."

My eyes widened in shock as she suddenly shoved my chest. Then she threw a leg over my lap and straddled me, her arms going around my neck. I relaxed against the couch, looking up at her with a growing smile. Her eyes practically sparkled at me, and I thought to myself again just how beautiful she was.

"You're beautiful," I told her because where was the fun in just keeping that to myself?

She grinned bashfully down at me, her arms circling my neck.

Before we could start anything, my phone rang. We both sighed in disappointment as I pulled it out of my pants pocket. I frowned at the number that I didn't recognize but was pretty sure came from the hotel.

"Hello?" I said cautiously.

"Mr. Thompson? My name is Margaret Jones. I'm head of the cleaning department at the hotel."

I frowned. "How did you get my number?"

There was a short silence, then came the tentative answer, "I called the office to talk to Matthew Thompson, but the secretary let me know he would be out of the office for the day. She gave me your phone number instead."

I rolled my eyes. Dad should have been back to work, not taking days off. And if he'd only done it so he could visit me, I was going to get mad. Besides, he'd left my place a long time ago, and even with the detour, I'd arrived back at the hotel already. So where was he?

And also, if the secretary was handing out my phone number, it was probably for something serious. My eyes narrowed as it sunk in that she said she was the head of the cleaning department, and I got a suspicion.

"What can I do for you, Margaret?" I asked, bracing myself.

"I'm calling to make a complaint," she said, and I closed my eyes in defeat.

"Let me guess," I said before she could continue. "My brother Mason had another party?"

"Yes, sir," she returned eagerly. "He set it up a couple of days ago and invited a lot of guests to the hotel. A lot of them are here for a few days extended stay."

Dammit. I step out to deal with an internal crisis and my brothers slack off. Or maybe it was his way of acting out after he found out the whole ruse with Dad's heart attack. I wondered what Kevin would do. He might just pack up and leave as was his usual habit.

"I'm sorry my brother has made a mess," I said, keeping my voice polite while internally wondering why I was apologizing for my brother's behavior. "I hope he didn't make too much trouble for your people..."

"It's not the mess that I am complaining about," she

said. "It was a bit much but it was taken care of. My problem is with the nudity."

My eyebrows shot up at that, and my gaze drifted over to Jessi, who was looking at me with curiosity.

"Nudity?" I repeated, not sure I wanted to know where this was going.

Jessi's eyes suddenly widened in recognition, and she slapped a hand over her mouth as she broke out into giggles. I arched an eyebrow at her but didn't complain because she looked too cute. I gave her a slight poke on the chin that had her giggling some more, then focused on the phone.

"Yes, sir," Margaret said. "Nudity. And only his, I might add, right around when the party was winding down. We can take care of a little mess, but…"

But Mason's wild ways were a little too much for the hotel to deal with. It was too much for me to deal with, too. Here I was, having a serious discussion about the love of my life, and I had to cut it off because my brother was getting himself into trouble again.

"Thank you for letting me know," I said after a beat. "I'll make sure to speak to my brother about his conduct at the hotel."

"Thank you, sir," she said, sounding satisfied.

I groaned when I cut off the call, dropping the phone on the couch beside me.

"What the fuck, Mason. Nudity?"

Jessi laughed again.

"Laura told me about that," she said with a snicker. "When she came here with Emily. She said she was there when it happened, and so were a lot of other maids there to clean up the mess. You might want to make sure no one caught it on camera or something."

I let out a heavy sigh. "Dad is going to be so annoyed with he finds out. And I'm the one that's going to have to deal with it because I'm the eldest."

It was another reason I'd stopped going to his parties. Even though he had lots of friends, because I was his older half-brother, I was automatically his guardian when he went overboard, which he tended to do often.

"Ugh. If this is him acting out, I'd hate to see what Kevin would do."

Jessi arched her eyebrows. "Acting out?"

I nodded. "From the news about Dad. It probably affected them as it would me, and I do know quite a bit about my brothers. I know Kevin would probably just up and leave if he were annoyed with Dad, so I hope they had their talk already."

"Aren't you going to go look for your brother?" she asked.

"Why the hell would I?" I retorted. "Besides, they only called for a complaint, not to go pick him up, so he must be at a room in the hotel somewhere already. I don't want to catch my little brother in the nude, thank you."

She giggled a little more. "You know, I don't think Laura minded the nudity all that much." She grinned. "I don't mind yours, either," she added cheekily.

I stayed still as she leaned closer to me to kiss me, her lips moving softly against mine before adding a little pressure. She took my lower lip between hers and sucked on it, nibbling on it with her teeth, then smoothing over it with a lick. When she pulled back, her gaze was full of desire, and it was enough to have me half hard instantly.

"I wouldn't mind a little of that, either," I said huskily.

I reached for her, pulling her into my arms, with one under her knees and the other behind her back, then stood up from the couch as I lifted her into my arms.

"Why don't we take this to the bedroom?" I asked as I made my way there. "The couch is a little small for me, but we can play on it some other time if you'd like."

She moaned and wrapped her arms around my neck. She leaned up to press a kiss to my chin, then another, and another, moving along my jaw. Then she nibbled a little on my ear, and my hands tightened on her as I tried not to trip.

"We're moving your things to my room tomorrow," I reminded her.

Jessi nodded and hummed her agreement, and I took it as enough. Carefully, I moved us over to the bed and set her down, then followed right after her.

I knew things weren't completely resolved. There was still the issue with my family, and with hers, and I would have to sit everyone down together shortly so I could explain things, but one thing was for certain; Jessi and I had a long future ahead of us. And I didn't want to miss a moment of it.

Like she echoed my thoughts, Jessi murmured, "This is our future now, you and me."

"Yeah," I whispered, pausing our little love session to bury my head in her shoulder and hug her to me. "The two of us, working together like we should have always been. Working out the snags instead of starting petty fights," I added with a little grin.

"And love," she added in a whisper. "Most of all love, Trent." She tugged on my hair until I lifted my head. "I've been waiting for it for so long, you have no idea just how long. And finally, it's here. It's going to change the both of us. I just know it."

I grinned as I ducked down for a kiss.

"I'm hoping it will," I admitted. "For the better, for both of us."

I leaned in for more kisses as we continued this small moment of our future, together.

ALSO BY SUMMER COOPER

DARK DESIRES
~ A billionaire dark romance series ~
Dark Desire
Dark Rules
Dark Secret
Dark Time
Dark Truth

BARRE TO BAR
~ A billionaire second chance series ~
Dancing With Lies
Dancing With Temptation
Dancing With Doubt
Dancing With Guilt
Dancing With Redemption

TWISTED INTENTION

~ A billionaire revenge romance series ~
Twisted Beauty
Twisted Love
Twisted Fate

Mafia's Obsession
~ A hot mafia romance series ~
Mafia's Dirty Secret
Mafia's Fake Bride
Mafia's Final Play

Screaming Demons
~ An MC romance series full of suspense ~
Rough Start
Rough Ride
Rough Choice
Rough Patch
Rough Return
Rough Road
Rough Trip
Rough Night
Rough Love

Standalone Contemporary Romance
Billionaire in Vegas
Billionaire Hunt
Billionaire's Game
Billionaire Retreat
Billionaire On Air

A Chance To Love
Somebody To Love
Not Mine To Love

252

Check out Summer's entire collection at
www.summercooper.com/books

ABOUT SUMMER COOPER

Thank you so much for reading. Without you, it wouldn't be possible for me to be a full-time author. I hope you enjoy reading my books as much as I do writing them.

Besides (obviously!) reading and writing, I also love cuddling my dogs, shouting at Alexa, being upside down (aka Yoga) and driving my family cray-cray!

Get in touch at
hello@summercooper.com
www.summercooper.com

facebook.com/summercooperauthor
instagram.com/summercooperauthor
goodreads.com/summercooper
bookbub.com/profile/summer-cooper

www.ingramcontent.com/pod-product-compliance
Lightning Source LLC
Chambersburg PA
CBHW051302210726
48287CB00002B/633